D1145287

'I'm not sleeping with you!'

Zachim tugged the horse blanket over the top of them. 'No, you're not. You're sleeping next to me. There's a big difference. We need to share body heat to keep warm. Relax and this will be a lot easier.'

Relax? Farah couldn't have been more tense if she'd tried. It had been a long time since she had been physically close to anyone, and all this bodily contact was messing with her head.

'This isn't right.'

'But kidnapping your Prince is fine?'

'Must you always have the last word?' she grumbled.

'I was going to ask the same of you.'

Not wanting to find him at all amusing, Farah curled herself into a tight ball to try and put distance between them. Self-sufficiency was a prized trait in the harsh desert climate, and Farah was proud that she could survive on her own if she had to. She wanted to point this out to the Prince, but that would involve speaking to him and she'd much rather pretend he wasn't there. She'd much rather pretend she was in her own bed than on the cold, hard ground, wrapped in the strong arms of her father's number one enemy.

With two university degrees and a variety of false career starts under her belt, **Michelle Conder** decided to satisfy her lifelong desire to write and finally found her dream job. She currently lives in Melbourne, Australia, with one super-indulgent husband, three self-indulgent (but exquisite) children, a menagerie of over-indulged pets, and the intention of doing some form of exercise daily. She loves to hear from her readers at michelleconder.com

Books by Michelle Conder

Mills & Boon Modern Romance

Prince Nadir's Secret Heir
The Most Expensive Lie of All
Duty at What Cost?
Living the Charade

The Chatsfield

Russian's Ruthless Demand

Dark, Demanding and Delicious

His Last Chance at Redemption

Scandal in the Spotlight

Girl Behind the Scandalous Reputation

**Visit the Author Profile page at
millsandboon.co.uk for more titles.**

HIDDEN IN THE SHEIKH'S HAREM

BY
MICHELLE CONDER

First published in Great Britain 2015
by Mills & Boon, an imprint of Harlequin (UK) Limited,
Eton House, 18-24 Paradise Road, Richmond, Surrey, TW9 1SR

© 2015 Michelle Conder

ISBN: 978-0-263-25893-6

Printed and bound in Great Britain
by CPI Antony Rowe, Chippenham, Wiltshire

HIDDEN IN THE
SHEIKH'S HAREM

For my family, with love. Always.
And to Bobo, shokran!

CHAPTER ONE

Prince Zachim Bakr Al-Darkhan tried not to slam the door as he left the palace apartment his half-brother was using for his brief visit but it wasn't easy. Nadir was being a cranky, stubborn hard-ass, refusing to take his rightful place as the next King of Bakaan, which left Zach in line for the job.

'Everything, all right, Highness?'

Damn; he was so preoccupied with what had just gone down he hadn't even sensed the elderly servant he'd known all his life waiting in the shadowed recess of the arched windows.

But, no, everything was not all right. Every day that passed without a leader made their people more and more uneasy. His father had only been dead for two weeks but already there were whispers of some of the more insurgent tribes gathering for 'talks'.

Yeah, like the Al-Hajjar tribe. Once their families had been rival dynasties, but two centuries ago the Darkhans had defeated the Hajjars in a brutal war, creating resentments that still remained. But Zach knew that the current leader of the tribe—Mohamed Hajjar—hated his father, not only because of their history, but because he held his father responsible for the death of his pregnant wife ten years ago. And probably his father had been partly responsible because, Allah knew, he had been responsible for the death of Nadir's mother for entirely different reasons.

The fact was their father had been a miserly tyrant who'd ruled through fear and had been ruthless when he didn't get his own way. As a result Bakaan was stuck in the dark ages, both in its laws and infrastructure, and it was going to be an enormous challenge to pull it into the twenty-first century.

A challenge that his brother was better suited to take on than Zach. And not just because Nadir was politically savvy with finely honed boardroom instincts, but also because it was his rightful place as the eldest son. With Nadir taking charge it would also free Zach up to do what he did best—creating and managing change at street level where he could do the most good.

Something he'd already started doing after his delicate mother had begged him to come home five years ago when Bakaan had been on the brink of civil war. The cause of the unrest had stemmed from a rogue publication started by someone in one of the mountain tribes detailing his father's failings and calling for change. There wasn't much in the publication Zach could argue with, but he'd done his duty and settled the unrest in his father's favour. Then, appalled at the state his country was in, he'd set aside his Western lifestyle and stayed, working behind the scenes to do what he could until his increasingly narcissistic and paranoid father had either seen sense or died. Death had come first and the only thing Zach felt was hollow inside. Hollow for the man who had only ever seen him as the spare to the throne, and not a very worthy one at that.

'Highness?'

'Sorry, Staph.' Zach shook off the memories he didn't want to delve into and started striding towards his own private wing of the palace, Staph quickstepping to keep pace with him. 'But, no, everything is not all right. My brother is proving to be stubborn.'

'Ah, he does not wish to return to Bakaan?'

No, he did not. Zach knew Nadir had good reason for not wanting to, but he also knew that his brother was born to be king, and that if Nadir could get past the bitterness he felt for their father, he would want to rule their small kingdom. Realising that Staph was having trouble keeping pace with him, Zach slowed. 'He has some other considerations to think of right now,' he hedged.

Like an infant daughter he hadn't known about and the mother he was set on marrying. Now, there had been a revelation to shock the hell out of Zach. Out of the two of them it was he who believed in love and marriage, while Nadir thought the concept had been created by the masses to counter boredom and a lack of productivity. Zach didn't believe that. He knew that one day he'd have a family who he'd treat a lot better than their old man had treated his.

In fact, he'd nearly proposed to a woman once; right before he'd been called home. Amy Anderson had ticked all his boxes—sophisticated, polished and blonde. Their courtship had gone smoothly and he still didn't know what had made him pull back. Nadir had been no help at the time, claiming that Zach had a tendency to choose women who were all wrong for him so that he didn't have to make a commitment at all.

Zach bid Staph goodnight and strode into his apartment. As if he'd ever take relationship advice from a confirmed bachelor. Or confirmed *ex*-bachelor, so it seemed.

Shedding his clothes on the way to the shower, he doused himself in steaming hot water before lying on his bed and willing himself to sleep. He'd agreed to meet his brother the following lunchtime so that Nadir could abdicate in front of the council but Zach was hoping he would see sense way before then.

When a message pinged into his phone, he immediately reached for the distraction and saw it was from a good friend he used to race superboats with, Damian Masters:

Check email for party invite. Ibiza. Also, just relented and gave Princess Barbie your private email address. Hope that's okay. D

Well, well, well. Zach wasn't one for all that 'signs and destiny' rubbish but he'd just been thinking about Amy—or 'Princess Barbie' as his friends had unhelpfully nick-named her—and now here she was.

Clicking onto his email list, he found hers and opened it.

Hi Zach, Amy here.
Long time, no chat. I hear you're going to Damian's party in Ibiza. I really hope to see you there. Catch up on old times perhaps??
Love Amy xxx

A wry smile crossed his face. If those question marks and kisses were any indication she wanted to do more than "catch up" on old times. But did he?

He laced his hands behind his head. He might not have thought of her much over the last five years, but what did that matter? It would be interesting to see her again and see how he felt. See if he still thought she should be the mother of his future children.

Almost distractedly he sent a short reply indicating that if he went to the party they would talk, but instead of feeling better he felt worse.

Sick of the thoughts batting back and forth inside his head and the restlessness that had invaded his usually up-beat attitude, he gave up on sleep, flung on jeans and a shirt, and headed out to the palace garage. Once there he jumped into an SUV and waved his security detail off as he turned the car towards the vast, silent desert beyond the city. Before he even knew he was thinking about it, he turned the car off-road and sped down one enormous sand dune after another, lit up in peaks and shadows by the light of the full moon.

Feeling his agitated mood ebb away, he let out a primal roar and pressed the accelerator flat to the floor.

Two hours later he disgustedly tossed the empty jerry can into the back of the car and swore profoundly. He hadn't realised how long he'd been out or how far he'd come and now he was stranded in the desert without any juice and no mobile phone reception.

No doubt his father would have put his impulsivity down to arrogance and his cavalier attitude to life. Zach just put it down to stupidity. He knew better than to head into the desert without a backup plan.

Hell.

Just then the soft whisper of movement had him turning as a dozen or so horsemen appeared on the horizon. Dressed all in black, with their faces covered by traditional *keffiyehs* to keep the sand out of their mouths and noses, he couldn't tell if they were friend or foe.

When all twenty of them lined up in front of him and sat motionless without saying a word, he thought probably foe.

Slowly, he walked his gaze over the line up. Probably he could take ten of them, given that he had a sword and a pistol with him. Probably he should try diplomacy first.

'I don't suppose one of you gentlemen has a jerry can full of petrol strapped to one of those fine beasts, do you?'

The creak of a leather saddle brought his attention back to the thickset stranger positioned at the centre of the group and who he had already picked as the leader. 'You are Prince Zachim Al Darkhan, pride of the desert and heir to the throne, are you not?'

Well, his father would probably argue with the antiquated 'pride of the desert' title, and he wasn't the direct heir, but he didn't think now was the time to quibble over semantics. And he already knew from his tone that the stranger with eyes of black onyx had figured out who he was. 'I am.'

'Well, this is fortuitous,' the old man declared and Zach could hear the smile in his voice even if he couldn't see it behind the dark cloth.

The wind picked up slightly but the night remained beautifully clear, full of stars and that big old moon that had beckoned him to leave the palace and burn up some of his frustrated energy on one of his favourite pastimes.

The old stranger leaned towards one of the other men, who then dismounted slowly from his horse. Of medium height and build, the younger man squared off in front of Zach, his legs braced wide. Zach kept his expression as impassive as he'd held it the whole time. If they were going to try and take him one at a time, this was going to be a cakewalk.

Then the other eighteen dismounted.

Okay, now that was more like it. Pity his weapons were in the car.

Farah Hajjar woke with a start and then remembered it was a full moon. She never slept well on a full moon. It was like an omen and for as long as she could remember she was always waiting for something bad to happen. And it had once. Her mother had died on the night of a full moon. Or, the afternoon of one, but Farah had been unable to sleep that night and she'd railed and cried at the moon until she'd been exhausted. Now it just represented sadness—sadness and pain. Though she wasn't twelve any more, so perhaps she should be over that. Like she should be over her fear of scorpions—not the easiest of fears to overcome when you lived in the desert where they bred like mice.

Rolling onto her side to get more comfortable, she heard the soft whinny of a horse somewhere nearby.

She wondered if it was her father returning from a weeklong meeting about the future of the country. Now that the horrible King Hassan was dead it was all he could talk about. That and how the dead king's son, the auto-cratic Prince Zachim, would probably rule the country in exactly the same way as the father had. The prince had led a fairy-tale existence, if the magazines Farah had read were true, before moving back to Bakaan full-time five years ago. As nothing had really changed in that time, she suspected her father was right about the prince—which was incredibly demoralising for the country.

Yawning, she heard the horses gallop off and wondered what was going on. Not that she would complain if her father would be gone for another day or two. Try as she might, she could never seem to get anything right with him, and Allah knew how hard she had tried. Tried and failed, because her father saw women as being put on the earth to create baskets and babies and not much else. In fact, he had remarried twice to try to sire a son and dis-carded both women when they had proved to be barren.

He couldn't understand Farah's need for independence and she couldn't understand why he couldn't understand it, why he couldn't accept that she had a brain and actu-ally enjoyed using it. On top of that he now wanted her to get married, something Farah vehemently did not want to do. As far as she could tell there were two types of men in the world: those who treated their wives well and those who didn't. But neither was conducive to a woman's over-all independence and happiness.

Her father, she knew, was acting from the misguided be-lief that all women needed a man's protection and guidance and she was fast running out of ways to prove otherwise.

She sighed and rolled onto her other side. It didn't help

that her once childhood friend had asked if he could court her. Amir was her father's right-hand man and he believed that a marriage between them was a perfect solution all round. Unfortunately, Amir was cut from the same cloth as her father, so Farah did not.

To add insult to injury, her father had just banned her from obtaining any more of her treasured Western magazines, blaming them for her 'modern' ideas. The truth was that Farah just wanted to make a difference. She wanted to do more than help supply the village with contraband educational material and stocks of medical supplies. She wanted to change the plight of women in Bakaan and open up a world for them that, yes, she had read about—but she knew she had zero chance of doing that if she were married.

Probably she had zero chance anyway but that didn't stop her from trying and occasionally pushing her father's boundaries.

Feeling frustrated and edgy, as if something terrible was about to happen, she readjusted her pillow and fell into an uneasy sleep.

The sense of disquiet stayed with her over the next few days, right up until her friend came racing up to where she was mucking out the camel enclosure and made it ten times worse.

'Farah! Farah!'

'Steady, Lila.' Farah set aside her shovel while her friend caught her breath. 'What's wrong?'

Lila gulped in air. 'You're not going to believe this but Jarad just returned from your father's secret camp and—' She winced as she took in another big breath of air, lowering her voice even though there was no one around to hear her but the camels. 'He said your father has kidnapped the Prince of Bakaan.'

CHAPTER TWO

FEELING HORRIBLY GUILTY that she had been enjoying her own time while her father was away, Farah raced to the ancient stables and saddled her beloved white stallion. If what Lila said was true then her father could face the death penalty and her heart seized.

As if he could sense her turmoil, Moonbeam whinnied and butted his head against her thigh as she saddled him. 'It's okay,' she said, knowing she was reassuring herself more than the horse. 'Just go like the wind. I don't have a good feeling about this.'

Riding into the secret camp a short time later, she reined in Moonbeam and handed him off to one of the guards to rub down. As it was dusk the camp was getting ready to bed down for the night, the tarpaulin tents shifting and sighing with the light breeze that lifted her *keffiyeh*. The camp was set up with mountains on one side and an ocean of desert on the other and she usually took a moment to appreciate the ochre tones in the dying embers of the evening sun.

Not tonight, though. Tonight she was too tense to think about anything other than hoping Lila was wrong.

'What are you doing here?' Amir asked curtly as she approached her father's tent, his arms folded across his chest, his face tense.

'What are you?' She folded her arms across her own

chest to show him she wasn't intimidated by his tough guy antics. He'd been her friend once, for Allah's sake.

'That's not your concern.'

'It is if what I just heard is true.' She took a deep breath. 'Please tell me it isn't.'

'War is men's business, Farah.'

'War?' The word squeaked out of her on a rush of air and she let out a string of choice words under her breath. Amir looked at her with the disapproving frown he wore ever since he had asked her father for her hand in marriage; the boy she had once played with, and who had taught her to use a sword when she'd been twelve and full of anger and despair over the death of her pregnant mother, seemingly long gone. 'So it's true.' Her voice dropped to barely a whisper. 'The Prince of Bakaan is here?'

Amir's lips tightened. 'Your father is busy.'

'Is he in there?'

She'd meant the prince but he'd misunderstood. 'He won't want to see you right now. Things are…tense.'

No kidding. You could have cut the air in the camp with a knife. 'How did this happen?' she demanded. 'You know my father is old and bitter. You're supposed to look out for him.'

'He is still leader of Al-Hajjar.'

'Yes, but—'

'Farah? Is that you?' Her father's voice boomed from inside the tent.

Farah's insides clenched. As much as her father's controlling and chauvinistic ways chafed—a lot—he was all she had in the world and she loved him. 'Yes, Father.' She swept past a disgruntled Amir and entered the plush interior of her father's retreat, lit from within by variously placed oil lamps.

The roomy tent was divided into sleeping and eating areas with a large bed at one end and a circle of cushions at the other. Worn rugs lined the floor to keep out the night-time chill and silk scarves were draped from the walls.

Her father looked tired as he sat amongst the cushions, the remnants of his evening meal set on a low table before him.

'What are you doing here, girl?'

Looking out for you, she wanted to say but didn't. Theirs had never been an overly demonstrative relationship even when her mother had been alive. Then, though, at least things had been happier and she'd tried so hard to get that feeling back in the years since.

Frown lines marred his forehead and his hands were clasped behind his broad back, his body taut. If she'd been a boy she would have been welcomed into this inner sanctum but she wasn't and maybe it was time she just accepted that. 'I heard that you have the Prince of Bakaan here,' she said in a 'please tell me it isn't true' voice.

He stroked his white beard, which she knew meant he was thinking about whether to answer her or not. 'Who told you?'

Farah felt as if a dead weight had just landed on her shoulders. 'It's true, then?'

'The information needs to be contained. Amir, see to it.'

'Of course.'

Not realising that Amir had followed her in, she turned to him, her eyes narrowing as she noticed that one of his eyes was blackened. 'Where did that come from?'

'Never mind!'

Farah wondered if it was from the prince and turned back to her father. 'But why? How?'

Amir stepped forward, his jaw set hard. 'Prince Zachim arrogantly assumed he could go dune driving in the middle of the night without his security detail.'

Ignoring him, Farah addressed her father. 'And?'

'And we took him.'

Just like that?

Farah cleared her throat, trying not to imagine the worst. 'Why would you do that?'

'Because I will not see another Darkhan take power and he is the heir.'

'I thought his older brother was the heir.'

'That dog Nadir lives in Europe and wants nothing to do with Bakaan,' Amir answered.

'That is beside the point.' She shook her head, still not comprehending what her father had done. 'You can't just... *kidnap a prince!*'

'When news gets out that Prince Zachim is out of the picture, the country will become more and more destabilised and we will be there to seize the power that has always been rightfully ours.'

'Father, the tribal wars you speak of were hundreds of years ago. And they won. Don't you think it's time to put the past to rest?'

'No, I do not. The Al-Hajjar tribe will never recognise Darkhan rule while I am leader and I can't believe my own daughter is talking like this. You know what he stole from me.'

Farah released a slow breath. Yes, the king's refusal to supply the outer regions of Bakaan with basic medical provisions, amongst other things, had inadvertently led to the death of her mother and her unborn brother—everything her father had held dear. Farah tried not to let her own misery at never quite being enough for her father rise up and consume her. She knew better than anyone that wanting love—relying on love—ultimately led to pain.

Her father continued on about everything else the Darkhans had stolen from them: land, privileges, freedom. Stories she'd heard at her bedtime for so long she sometimes heard them in her sleep. Truth be told, she actually agreed with a lot of what her father said. The dead King of

Bakaan had been a selfish, controlling tyrant who hadn't cared a jot for his people. But kidnapping Prince Zachim was not, in her view, the way to correct past wrongs. Especially when it was an offence punishable by imprisonment or death.

'How will this bring about peace and improve things, Father?' She tried to appeal to his rational side but she could see that he had a wild look in his eyes.

Her father shrugged. 'The country won't have a chance of overthrowing the throne with him on it. He's too powerful.'

Yes, Farah had heard that Prince Zachim was successful and powerful beyond measure. She had also heard he was extremely good-looking, which had been confirmed by the many photos she'd seen of him squiring some woman or another to glamorous events. Not that his looks were important on any level!

She rubbed her brow. 'So what happens now? What was the Bakaan council's response?'

For the first time since she'd walked in, her father looked uncertain. He rose and paced away from her, his hands gripped behind his back. 'They don't know yet.'

'They don't know?' Farah's eyebrows knit together. 'How can they not know?'

'When I am ready to reveal my plans, I will do so.' Which told Farah that he didn't actually have a plan yet. 'But this is not something I am prepared to discuss with you. And why are you dressed like that? Those boots are made for men.'

Farah scuffed her steel-capped boots against the rug. She'd forgotten that she still wore old clothes from working with the camels, but seriously, they were going to discuss her clothing while he held the most important man in the country hostage? 'That's not important. I—'

'It is important if I say it is. You know how I feel.'

'Yes, but I think there are more...pressing things to discuss, don't you?'

'Those things are in play now. There is nothing that can be done.'

A sudden weariness overcame him and he flopped back onto the cushions, his expression looking suspiciously like regret. Farah's heart clenched. 'Is he...is he at least okay?' She cringed as visions of the prince beaten up came into her head. She knew that would only make things worse—if that was even possible.

'Apart from the son of a dog refusing to eat, yes.'

'No doubt he thinks the food is poisoned,' she offered.

'If I wanted him dead, I'd use my sword,' her father asserted.

'How very remiss of him.' Fortunately her sarcasm went over his head, but it didn't escape Amir, who frowned at her. She rolled her eyes. She knew he thought she overstepped the boundaries with her father but she didn't care. She couldn't let her father spend his last years in prison—or, worse, die.

'Perhaps that is the answer,' Amir mused. 'We kill him and get rid of the body. No one could pin his death on us.'

Farah gave him a fulminating glare. 'I can't believe you said that, Amir. Apart from the fact that it's completely barbaric, if the palace found out, they would decimate our village.'

'No one would find out.'

'And no one is going to die, either.' She shoved her hands on her hips and thought about how to contain the testosterone in the room before it reached drastic levels. 'I will go and see him.'

'You will not go near him, Farah,' her father ordered. 'Dealing with the prisoner is a man's job.'

Wanting to point out that her father was doing a hatchet job of it if the prince was refusing to eat, Farah wisely kept her mouth shut. Instead she decided to take matters into her own hands.

'Where are you going?'

She stiffened as Amir called out to her in a commanding tone. Slowly she pivoted back around to face him. 'To get something to eat,' she said tightly. 'Is that okay?'

He had the grace to look slightly uncomfortable. 'I would like to speak with you.'

She knew he was waiting on her answer as to whether she would accept his courtship but she wasn't in the mood to face his displeasure when she told him no. 'I don't have anything to say to you right now,' she informed him.

His jaw tensed. 'Wait for me outside.'

Farah smiled sweetly. Like that was going to happen!

Quickly stepping out of the tent, she took a moment to pull her headdress lower and bent her head to shield her eyes against the setting sun. The air temperature had already dropped and the nearby tents flapped in the increasing wind. She looked for signs of a storm but found nothing but a pale blue sky. That didn't mean one wasn't coming. In the desert they came out of nowhere.

Deciding not to waste time on food, she stomped off to the only tent that had a guard posted outside, anger rolling through her. Anger at her father for his outrageous actions and anger at the prince himself—the lowly offspring of the man who had inadvertently caused her mother's death and changed her once-happy life forever.

She tried to get her emotions under control but it felt like she was fighting a losing battle. Still, she needed to remain calm if she was going to work out a way to get her father out of this mess before he did something even more insane—like listen to Amir!

CHAPTER THREE

ZACHIM SHIFTED HIS hands and feet and felt the ropes chafe his wrists and one of his ankles where it had slipped beneath his jeans. His stomach growled.

Ordinarily he wouldn't say he was a man who angered easily. Three days in this hellhole at the hands of a bunch of mountain heathens had ensured that his temper not only festered, but also boiled and blistered as well. And it wasn't just directed outwards. It had been stupid to drive so far from the city without alerting anyone as to where he was going.

He rubbed the ropes binding his wrists against the small sharp stone hidden in his lap. He'd picked it up when he'd 'fallen' during a toilet break the day before. Since refusing to eat, his ropes had not been checked, which was to his advantage, because it had taken that long to work through the thick layers, but he was just about there. Once his hands were free it would be a simple matter to untie his ankles and get the hell out of there.

He leant his head against the solid wooden post he was secured to by a length of rope circling his waist. It allowed him enough room to lie down on the dusty ground but that was it. What he wouldn't give for the comforts of his soft bed back at the palace. Ironic when he considered that three days ago he'd been looking for a way to leave the stifling walls of the place.

Be careful what you wish for, he thought grimly.

He wondered what had happened in his absence and how his brother was dealing with the fallout from his disappearance. He also wondered why he hadn't heard any search helicopters fly overhead.

Flexing stiff muscles that had been bound for too long, he tried to ignore the fact that his stomach was trying to eat itself. He'd been in worse situations during his stint in the army, though he wouldn't wish that on anyone. Okay, maybe he'd wish it on Mohamed Hajjar and his pompous second-in-command who thought himself mightier than a prince.

The sound of footsteps pausing at the entrance of his tent brought his head up and he shoved the sharp rock beneath him. When the flap was raised he feigned sleep, hoping that whoever had arrived would leave quickly so he could get on with sawing at his bindings. If they were checked now there was no way the person wouldn't notice what he'd been up to.

With his senses on high alert, he listened to the sound of the soldier's footfalls. A lightweight, he decided. About one hundred and twenty pounds. Someone he could take easily if it came to that. Unable to smell food, he wondered what the soldier wanted. It was too soon for a toilet break so he kept his features impassive. Whoever it was had gone a few too many rounds with a camel, by the smell of them.

'I know you're not asleep,' a low, sexy voice murmured, sending ripples of awareness across his skin. Hell, that was some voice the soldier had, and he slowly peeled his eyes open, curiosity getting the better of him. He took in black steel-capped boots and combat trousers and moved up the slender figure from the dusty midthigh-length tunic that covered a small pair of breasts plumped up by rigidly folded arms. His gaze lifted to an unsmiling but feminine face that was shadowed by the tribe's traditional red-checked *keffiyeh*. Not a guy, then—a relief, given his body's instant reaction to the voice.

'And I know you're not a man even though you're dressed like one. I didn't know Hajjar allowed women in his army of rebels.'

She stiffened slightly. 'Who I am is not important.'

Zach leant his head back against the pole and watched her. She was quite petite overall and was probably less than one twenty, now that he got a good look at her. Maybe one ten, he assessed with the clinical precision left over from his army days.

The taut silence lengthened between them but he knew it wouldn't take her long to break it. Her energy was twitchy despite her outwardly cool composure.

'I want to make a deal with you,' she finally said.

A deal?

The rage he'd been feeling earlier that had been eclipsed momentarily by curiosity returned with full force. He controlled it but barely. 'Not interested.' He knew Nadir would be looking for him—and if he didn't get here soon he had his own escape plans—and then he'd bring hell down on Mohamed Hajjar for holding him like this.

The girl's eyes flashed darkly before she subdued them. 'You haven't heard what I'm offering yet.'

'If you wanted to gain my attention you should have worn less.' He raked her body with his impassive gaze. 'A lot less. Possibly nothing at all, although even then I'm not sure you have what it takes to hold my interest.'

A lie, because for some reason she already had it. But his taunt had hit its mark if her little gasp was anything to go by.

'My father is right. You're a lowly dog who doesn't deserve to rule our country.'

'Your father?'

Farah Hajjar? Mohamed's daughter? Well, well, wasn't

that interesting? His gaze raked her again and he nearly smiled when he caught the self-disgusted look that crossed her face at her mistake. He hadn't expected the old guy to send his daughter to do his bidding. Was he hoping Zach would somehow be seduced into making a deal? If he was, he was going to be disappointed because, despite his reaction to her voice, Zach had never been attracted to Bakaani women. A shrink would no doubt tell him that it was because of the amount of arranged marriages his father had tried to foist on him. But Zach just preferred blondes. 'I didn't think your father considered himself a part of Bakaan but it's nice to know that he still does.'

'He...' She stopped and Zach could see she was trying to rein her temper in. She took a deep breath and slammed her hands on her hips, drawing his attention to their feminine curve. *Not going to help, sweetheart.*

'If you agree to let our region formally separate from Bakaan,' she said, 'I'll let you go.'

'*You'll* let *me* go?'

He laughed and she paced away from him, her stride long, and he realised she wasn't as small as he'd first assumed: maybe five-seven, five-eight. She stopped abruptly, facing him. 'Your family has suppressed our people for long enough.'

Now that was something he couldn't argue with. He didn't condone how his father had ruled Bakaan, and he'd even considered launching a coup against him himself, but his mother would have been devastated. 'I haven't done anything to the people of Bakaan.' But he couldn't allow her tribe to secede from the kingdom because others might follow and the country would get picked over by their neighbours, seeking to secure Bakaan's oil reserves for themselves.

'You haven't done anything *for* them either,' she countered, 'even though you've been back and have controlled the army for the last five years.'

'And when was the last time that army attacked any of your people, or any other country, for that matter?' Zach bit out, surprised that her attitude had got to him.

'You're saying you're responsible for peace?' She scoffed.

'I'm saying that, for all your big talk, your father has potentially instigated a war by his current actions. Not me.' Her face paled at that and his eyes narrowed. 'Something to think about, *sweetheart*, before you run off at the mouth with your uneducated accusations!'

'You only think they're uneducated because I'm a woman. I know more than you think, *Your Highness*.'

She loaded his title with as much derision as she could muster, which was a pretty impressive amount. But her spunk only irritated him more. 'A woman?' he taunted. 'I've known skunks that smell better than you. I would advise against marketing the scent. It's not all that appealing.'

Her eyes flashed darkly in the dying light. 'As if I would want to appeal to you,' she returned scathingly.

Zach nearly laughed at her haughty tone. He'd yet to come across a woman who didn't want to appeal to him. Good genes, a good bank account and what sounded like a good title went a long way to impressing the female population. He raised his hands in the air and cocked an eyebrow. 'Untie my hands, little heathen, and I'll soon change your mind.'

He almost heard her teeth grind together from across the room at his suggestive tone and, just as she was about to launch into what he could only imagine was another cutting admonition of his character, the tent flap was once again pushed aside and Hajjar's second-in-command sauntered in, bearing a dish of food. The smell hit Zach instantly and made his stomach curl in on itself.

Obviously surprised to see Mohamed's daughter, he pulled up short. 'What are you doing here?' he bit out.

Zach saw her chin snap up and her eyes shoot daggers. 'I can handle this, Amir,' she murmured icily.

'No, you can't.'

She responded in hushed tones and Zach avidly followed their furiously whispered interaction. She clearly had a personal relationship with the soldier and for some inexplicable reason he was disappointed.

Not wanting to dwell on why that was, he focused on the soldier's face. He wasn't at all happy with whatever it was she was saying but he clearly lacked the *baydot* to do anything about it. Idiot. All she needed was a sound kissing and she'd see reason.

A sound kissing?

He nearly chocked at the absurdity of the thought. His ancestors might have behaved that way, but since when did he think kissing a woman into submission was an acceptable mode of conduct for a man? And who would want to kiss this smelly little spitfire anyway?

Disgusted with his interest in their argument, he drew up his knees and used their distraction to work at his bindings.

Too soon the woman won and took the bowl of food from the soldier's hands. Needing more time alone, Zach goaded him by asking where he'd misplaced his *baydot*. The soldier stiffened. So did the spitfire.

She whirled on him, all fire and ice. Maybe 'spitfire' was too tame a word to describe her. She was more like a wild little cat with her dark, almond-shaped eyes and pursed lips.

'Come, Farah.'

The girl rounded on the other man and, for all that Zach didn't like him, he felt himself wince for the guy. 'He's just trying to rile you,' she bit out.

Not stupid, then, Zach mused with reluctant admiration.

'He is dangerous,' the soldier returned. And he should know, since it had taken six of them to subdue him.

'And tied up,' she pointed out impatiently. 'Which I have no plans to change.' But Zach did and he felt another coil of rope give as he put more pressure on it.

'What *are* your plans?'

Fascinated by the changed tension in the air, Zach stilled his movements. He sensed there was more behind that question than met the eye. The girl obviously did, too, but her scrunched brow indicated that she didn't understand the meaning behind his question.

He wants in your pants, sweetheart, if he hasn't been there already.

She released a slow breath. 'Just give me five minutes here. I'll meet you in the dinner tent.'

Slightly mollified, the soldier nodded tersely. He sneered at Zach before stalking out of the tent, letting the flap drop back loudly into place.

She stared at it, brooding.

'Trouble in paradise, little cat?' Zach offered, as if they were old friends taking tea together.

His question snapped her out of her reverie and she marched back to him. 'Be quiet. And don't call me that.'

'I thought you wanted me to speak.'

She glanced down at the small metal bowl in her hand and frowned. 'What I want is for you to eat.'

Zach's stomach agreed with her. 'I'm not hungry.'

She scoffed. 'What is the point of starving yourself? You'll die.'

'So nice of you to care.'

'I don't.'

Her condescending attitude and lack of respect annoyed the hell out of him and he was starting to get some inkling as to the reasoning behind his ancestors' methods of subduing a woman. He wouldn't mind having this one bow down at his feet and acknowledge his superior position to hers. 'You know, your father might want to send someone with better interpersonal skills to plead for leniency next time,' he suggested testily.

Damn, but the urge to have this man bow and scrape at her feet was so strong Farah nearly pulled her small dagger out from inside the hidden pocket in her tunic and made him do it. His attitude was truly irritating.

As were those piercing golden eyes. Lion's eyes. They said so much and nothing at all, just stared back at her as if he knew something that she didn't. With the few days' worth of beard growth covering his angular jaw, those implacable eyes made him seem harshly masculine and deeply imposing even though he was sitting on the ground. The tightly coiled energy he emanated made her think of a cobra about to strike. Or an eagle about to take flight and rip its prey to shreds. He wore a dusty black shirt that stretched across broad shoulders and jeans that hugged what looked to be powerful thighs, the muscles bunching periodically when he looked at her.

She'd known he was incredibly good-looking from the magazine pictures she'd seen, but with his aristocratic features, wide mouth and pitch-black, neatly cropped hair, he was something else in the flesh. Not that she cared.

'I have not come to plead for leniency,' she assured him.

'Lucky.' His eyes trapped hers in a challenging stare. 'Because when I get out of here I have no intention of giving it.'

Her mouth twisted. 'Perhaps you need a little longer to think about your position,' she suggested, glancing pointedly at his bound hands.

'Perhaps I do,' he drawled carelessly.

Oh, but he was getting under her skin! She stared him down for another few minutes and then gave up. This wasn't a contest, even though he seemed determined to turn it into one. 'Nevertheless…' she began, pausing when his hands clenched in his lap yet again. She made a mental note to check his bindings before she left. The last thing she needed was to return him damaged. It would only fare worse for her father. 'You are not going to die on my watch.'

'And there I was thinking that our plans weren't in alignment.' He smiled and Farah felt an unfamiliar jolt of heat deep in her belly. His teeth gleamed whitely against his dark stubble and she scowled to cover her unexpected reaction. The man was dangerous; his cavalier attitude in the face of his imprisonment was proof enough of that even before one took in the breadth of those shoulders.

Determined not to be intimidated, Farah crouched down in front of the high and mighty Prince of Bakaan. She watched as he blatantly worked his gaze over her from head to toe and for a moment she couldn't move; a horrible urge to arch her spine and thrust her breasts out for his inspection making her nipples pull tight.

Rocked to her core by the inclination she noticed his eyelids had lowered to half-mast making her feel both hot and cold all over, her sense of danger heightened like never before.

The silence between them lengthened and Farah became aware that her breathing was shallow and that her clothing felt rough against her skin. She couldn't seem to drag her eyes away from his perfectly proportioned mouth and, as if he sensed her inner turmoil, one corner of it tilted knowingly. More annoyed than ever, she shifted her weight to the balls of her feet, slowly raised the bowl between them and offered it to him.

He didn't look at the food. Instead his golden eyes held hers in such a way that made her discomfort levels hit an all-time high. 'If you're so interested in getting me to eat, then you feed me, my feral little cat.'

Feral little cat? The shock of those soft words had Farah rocking back on her heels as feminine pride kicked in. She might not look her best but she was hardly feral! And as for feeding him... She felt steam rising out of her ears. Even tied up and at her mercy he assumed the superior position. 'I have no intention of feeding you,' she snapped.

He gave a soft, deep chuckle that took up residence in the pit of her stomach. 'Well, there goes that fantasy.'

Farah's mouth tightened at the taunt. He'd already made it clear he thought she was lacking in the female department so his comments could only be to try and throw her off. Though to what end, other than to rile her, she didn't know.

It was obvious he didn't believe she would take him up on his challenge to feed him—and normally she wouldn't even think of doing so, but there was something about this insolent prince that rubbed her up the wrong way. Plus, she'd dealt with dusty, stubborn camels her whole life so one dirty, scruffy male would be no different. Involuntarily her eyes dropped to his body. It was difficult to see the full extent of his physique in his current position but there was no doubt he emanated a masculine power she hadn't come across before. Or had never noticed.

She glanced at his hands and the rope around his waist that kept him tethered to the post. The sense of menace and danger that cloaked him made her think twice about her next actions while the wicked glint in his eyes goaded her on. But it wasn't as if he could actually do anything to her, tied as he was.

A shiver went through her anyway and she lifted her chin. 'If I feed you, will you eat?'

One dark eyebrow lifted lazily and dense ebony lashes lowered slowly to shield his eyes. 'You'll need to get closer to find out.'

Farah ignored the sudden leap of her pulse at his words. Better just to get this over and done with and she'd have one thing accomplished. And wasn't it true that a man with a full stomach had a better disposition than one with an empty one? Maybe then he'd be more amenable to seeing reason.

Besides, she had something to prove. This was nothing more than a classic power play and she would not let him see that he intimidated her. Not that he did, exactly; it was just that any animal handler knew that you approached an unknown beast with caution. Particularly a large, predatory one.

Deciding that, like cleaning the privy, thinking about the deed was worse than actually doing it, Farah clenched her jaw and dug the tips of her fingers into the fragrant meat dish. She had to shuffle even closer to him and his male scent rose to mingle with the food. Logically he should have smelt like a pair of damp old socks. He didn't. He smelt of man and sweat and heat.

Heat?

What did heat even smell like?

That was about as relevant to her current objective as the shape of his mouth. Quickly, before she could change her mind, she scooped out a portion of meat and rice, careful to keep the bowl close to catch any drips, and leaned forward onto the balls of her feet before raising her fingers to his mouth.

In this position she was almost straddling him and she flushed hotly as unexpected images of the two of them naked and entwined came into her head. A year ago she'd seen a sexy magazine spread of a man and a woman pretending to make love. She'd felt a momentary jolt of curiosity at seeing them but it was nothing compared to the jolt she was feeling now. She'd always viewed sex as a means of procreation, not pleasure. So why had her mind transplanted the skimpily clad models in the magazine with the two of them? It was so clear she could almost picture the prince's powerful body lying beneath her own; she could almost see herself sitting astride him; could almost feel the press of his ribs against her inner thighs. She squeezed them together unconsciously and heat bloomed there, catching her off guard.

The walls of the tent seemed to draw in around her as she fought to contain her body's visceral reaction to her thoughts and she frowned as the prince's firm lips remained resolutely closed. Exasperated, she lifted her eyes to his, the angry tirade she was about to unleash on him dying on her tongue as he chose that moment to lean forward and draw the rice and meat—and her fingers—inside his warm mouth.

As soon as her fingers slipped inside his lips, his tongue curled around them to claim the food. She felt its warm, thick moistness and shuddered at the rush of liquid heat between her legs and the tingling sensation that caused her nipples to tighten. She'd never experienced anything like this and she couldn't tear her eyes from his.

Dimly aware that she was all but panting, she was completely mesmerised by the way he licked and sucked on her fingers, some deep part of her consciousness trying to tell her that her fingers were now well and truly clean. Still she allowed him to linger, another part of her consciousness urging her to replace her fingers with her mouth. It was so overpowering it was all she could do not to lean in and...

Realising she was about to topple into him, she felt a fire rise up to consume her face and jerked back. Before she could remove her fingers, however, he gripped her wrist and stroked his tongue in between the webbing.

'I think I missed a bit,' he murmured in a rough voice that worked like a sanding tool over her sensitive skin. His tongue flicked back and forth, back and forth, in a purely sensual exploration, before gently biting down on her sensitive palm.

A small whimper escaped her lips and her fingers curled against his beard-roughened face, her body swaying toward his. Almost absently she was aware that a warning voice had started clanging inside her brain but his hand was pressing hers closer. His hand that was…that was…

By Allah! Farah's eyes flew to his as it finally registered that his hands were free, only to find him staring into hers with a knowing gleam. Immediately she tried to wrench herself free and the small metal bowl hit the dirt as she valiantly pushed against him. Unfortunately he was on her quicker than lightning could fork into the ground and she was on her back before she had time to blink.

Slightly winded from the way he tossed her onto the ground, Farah twisted away from him to scream, but the back of her head hit the dirt as his large hand clamped over her mouth. 'Oh, no, you don't. There will be no calling the cavalry just yet, sweetheart.'

Farah squirmed beneath the weight of his upper body and knew it was futile to push against him. He was too strong. And it wasn't just from lean, hard-packed muscle either. One look into his furious face and she could see that he'd leashed his rage so successfully she hadn't realised how deep it ran. Although she *should* have, and perhaps she *would* have, if she hadn't been stupidly distracted by his masculinity and her own rioting hormones.

Knowing she could never throw him from this angle, she tried desperately to get her hands beneath her tunic to her hidden dagger that had saved her skin a few times in the past. Admittedly those times had been from snakes and scorpions, but hadn't she already noted that this man was just as dangerous as any predator? Having learnt how to use a dagger and to fight with a sword when she was younger, Farah knew just where to threaten him with it so that he'd let her go. But it was as if he could read her mind because he caught her wandering hand in his and brought it over her head.

Frantic at the ease with which he contained her, she desperately curled her fingers towards his skin in the hope of causing some damage but he pressed the hand against her mouth more firmly and brought her eyes to his.

'Scratch me, little cat, and I'll scratch you back,' he growled close to her ear.

Farah paused at the menace in those words but then she realised that he would have to let her go to scratch her so she didn't care. She kicked out, catching his shin with the solid point of one boot, and scratched at his wrists at the same time.

'Damn it to hell!' He cursed softly and stretched her arms high to breaking point, pinning her legs down with one of his. Farah moaned behind his hand. She was struggling to draw oxygen into her lungs and was thankful when he adjusted his palm a little to ease her growing dizziness.

'Follow my instructions and I won't hurt you,' he promised.

Ha! As if she believed that. His family had been hurting the people of Bakaan for centuries and tyranny ran in his veins as surely as the blood she'd just drawn on his wrist.

The weight of him felt like an anvil slowly crushing her chest and Farah was just wondering how she could lever her legs to help dislodge him when she felt him go still above her.

'Damn it, keep still.'

His rough tone compelled her to stop fighting him and she was completely unprepared when he flipped her onto her stomach. Before she could pull in another breath, he had her hands wrapped in the same rope that should still have bound his own.

Sand coated her eyelashes and filled her nose and she tried to turn her head before she suffocated. It was then that she felt his hand smoothing over her bottom and fear turned her as cold as stone. Surely he wasn't going to… going to…?

'Easy, little spitfire.' He brought his hand up to the side of her face and she felt the cool blade of her dagger flat against her cheek. 'Quite a nice little piece. I could have used this a couple of days ago,' he said mockingly. 'Do you even know how to use it?'

Trust him to think that she wouldn't be able to handle a knife. Her eyes flashed with annoyance but she wasn't going to tell him anything. Not that she could with his hand pressed against her mouth. But she could still make sounds, she realised, and although she couldn't hear anyone walking outside she knew there was a guard nearby. If he heard something, he'd come running.

Squirming beneath him, she tugged against the rope and screamed behind his hand.

Immediately his thumb and forefinger pinched her nose and her ears popped as she tried to force the sound out of her lungs. She thrashed her head from side to side even though she knew it was futile.

'This is how it's going to go,' he murmured when she finally exhausted herself. 'I'm going to take my hand away from your mouth and you're going to stay quiet.'

Farah listened but she knew there was no way she was going to follow his orders.

'If you don't, you'll surely bring the guard in from outside and I'll be forced to kill him with *your* dagger.'

Fear kept her immobile. It was one thing to risk her own life but she'd never risk another person's.

Roughly he pulled her to her feet. 'Nod if you're going to comply.'

CHAPTER FOUR

FOR A MOMENT Zach thought he was going to have to knock her out cold and he didn't want to do that. In order to get out of the camp, he needed her to lead him to the horses without drawing too much attention to them.

Fortunately she had no idea how important she was to his escape and she nodded curtly. Slowly Zach drew his hand back and she immediately pressed her lips together as if he'd hurt them. Probably he had. She'd fought like a little wild thing and he was surprised at how strong she was. He was surprised at how slender and soft she had felt beneath him as well, and at how beautiful her face was— oh, not classically, like the faces of many of the women he'd dated, but there was something about the slant of her cheekbones and those bottomless brown eyes that made him want to sink into them. Her smooth skin and sexy-as-sin mouth didn't hurt, either.

With her *keffiyeh* having come off during their struggle, he ran his eyes over her heart-shaped face and down the long dark plait that rested just above small jutting breasts. She was dishevelled and in need of a bath, her proud little chin tilted upwards as if she wanted to tell him to go to hell, but still he wanted to hear her make that soft little hitch in her voice she'd made when he'd sucked on her fingers.

Hell of a time to get a hard-on, oh mighty pride of the desert.

He looked her over. 'Do you have any other weapons, my little Zenobia?' he asked dulcetly, unwinding the rope from her slender wrists.

She rubbed at them and, even though it was nearly completely dark inside the tent, he could still read her fury and the desire to best him in her eyes. 'As if I'd tell you that.'

'If you don't, I'll be forced to search you.'

'No!' The sharp little word sprang from her lips like an Olympian off the starter's block. 'I don't.'

Zach nearly laughed at the desperation behind her words and wondered if she was afraid of him or afraid of the unexpected chemistry that had ignited between them.

Chemistry he needed to ignore.

'Come.'

Her chin shot up again and she tossed her head like a mare that was being pulled too hard at the bit. 'I'm not going anywhere with you.'

Zach smiled grimly. 'You are. You're about to walk me out of here and take me to the horses. If anyone stops us, you will tell them that you are taking me to your father. You'll then lead me by this rope that will look like it is binding my hands until we get there.'

He could almost hear her thoughts running wild, trying to take an alternate route. He yanked her against him and ignored her shocked gasp and the way his palm fit snuggly around the curve of her bottom. He had a moment of questioning his decision, of second-guessing his plan, but he really had no other option. And he'd let her go as soon as they got to the horses. In the meantime, she needed to know that he wasn't about to cop any attitude from her. 'Sound the alarm and I'll kill anyone who stops us.'

The desert was already freezing and he could hear the rising wind beating at the sides of the tent and making a hell of a racket. He had no idea how far Mohamed Hajjar's camp lay from civilisation but he knew it was going to be a long night.

Bending down, he retrieved a length of rope and coiled it around his wrists. He knew an observant guard would notice that his ankles were no longer bound but he was hoping the closing darkness would prevent anyone from noticing that before they got to the horses. Of course, he'd much prefer a high-powered vehicle to climb into, but in the three days he'd been held hostage he hadn't once heard the sound of an engine.

Zach positioned Farah just to the side so he could observe her expression. 'Okay, my little warrior queen, let's go.'

'I'm not your anything.' She kept her face averted but he saw the betraying tremble of her lower lip. For all her attitude, she was afraid of him. Not something he was going to allay even though he had never hurt a woman in his life. Of course, he'd never had cause to before now. Women loved him and he loved them—a much more desirable arrangement than this one.

'Move.' He positioned himself slightly in front of her but, rather than her grabbing his hands, he grabbed hers, laying the small dagger against her inner arm so that she knew who was in charge. 'And don't rush it.'

When she lifted the tent flap he blew out a relieved breath that her boyfriend didn't appear to be in the vicinity.

The nearby guard was, though, and he immediately came to attention when he saw them. He asked Farah if everything was okay and when she hesitated Zach pressed the tip of her sharp dagger against her wrist.

'Fine,' she said through clenched teeth.

'We'll have to brush up on your acting skills but good enough for now,' Zach whispered against her ear and got another whiff of camel. He grimaced and wondered whether she'd been rolling around with them.

'You can't get away. There's a storm brewing.'

Zach had already clocked the incoming storm and his eyes scanned the camp. Many of the men were still filling their stomachs around the campfire and the remaining ones were busy securing the tents against the rising wind. 'I know. Perfect cover.'

She stopped and he nearly ran into her. 'I won't do it,' she hissed out of the side of her mouth.

'Your father will mourn your death, no doubt.'

'You won't kill me.'

Zach crowded her from behind. 'It would be a mistake to underestimate what I would or would not do right now. Have you forgotten who my father was?'

'Pig.' The word was spat towards the sand.

Exactly. Zach urged her forward. 'I'm glad we understand each other. Now, walk and none of your men will die. Hopefully.'

Farah brushed at the strands of her hair that had come loose from her struggles with the prince and which now blew uncontrollably around her face. She was so angry with herself for being duped, she could spit. No doubt this would reinforce for her father that women were best left to domestic chores and had no place getting involved in the business of men. Right now she had to agree because it was her own stupidity that had got her into this mess. As if reading her mind, the hateful prince leaned in close again, his warm breath stirring the loose strands of hair at her temple. 'Don't feel bad about aiding my escape. If it had been anyone else, I would have been forced to kill him.'

That thought gave her little comfort. She had made a mistake and didn't know how to fix things. And she always knew how to fix things. It was her calling card. Everyone in the village came to her when there was trouble. And now she'd caused the trouble—or at least exacerbated it before a solution could be found.

Focusing on the biting cold wind against her face, she willed one of the men around her to notice that something was amiss. Other than a cursory glance, they didn't question her. They trusted her. Trusted her, and she was about to let them down. A well of emotion rose up in her throat and self-pitying tears filled her eyes.

'Stop here.'

The prince's words were low and with a start Farah realised they had already reached the horses. As if sensing her presence, her big stallion trotted over.

'By Allah, he's a monster,' the prince murmured appreciatively.

One of the men had put him in a halter and blanket to ward off the cold and as soon as he reached them he stretched his nose out to her, as if seeking a treat.

'Yours?'

She knew from the tone of his voice that he was going to steal him and she shoved at Moonbeam's muzzle to try and push him away.

At the same time a cry went up from across the camp. It was Amir calling her name; the prince tensed. Relief flooded Farah and she pushed harder at Moonbeam to get him to go. Typically male, he didn't listen so she yelled at him.

More shouts rung out around them and Farah could hear the heavy sound of feet pounding the sand as her father's men rallied. Giving up all pretence that he was still captured, the prince shoved her through the gate, her scream lost on the driving wind. Then suddenly hard hands spanned her waist and her eyes snapped back to the prince's. She saw a moment of indecision cross his face, then she was being lifted, and she instinctively raised her leg to swing it over Moonbeam's neck before she thought better of it.

Seconds later the prince vaulted on behind her and kicked her stallion into action. Being herd animals, the remaining horses fretted and the prince used this to his advantage, wheeling around behind them and forcing them out of the gate.

Before she knew it they were in full flight and all Farah could do was grab Moonbeam's mane as the prince reached around her for the halter and raced them straight into the dark heart of the incoming storm.

Hours later, wet, filthy and exhausted, the prince stopped the now plodding horse. Farah would have slipped from Moonbeam's back if the man behind her hadn't tightened his arm around her waist, the steel-like muscles bunching beneath her breasts as they had so often done over the past few hours.

Some time ago, when the storm had hit hard, he had stopped and pulled off his shirt to tie around Moonbeam's eyes and nose to shield him from the worst of the swirling dust. He'd then cut the bottom of her tunic to make two coverings to keep as much of the sand off their faces, as well.

Feeling wretched, with sand coating every part of her cold, wet body, Farah could have cried with relief when she glanced up to see a rocky incline in front of them.

Jumping down from the stallion's back, the prince reached up and tugged her off, unceremoniously dragging her and her horse under the shelter. It wasn't much, just a narrow crevice really, but it was facing away from the wind. When he released her arm, she swayed and he held her while her legs worked to keep her upright.

Carefully she unwrapped her makeshift headdress and shook it out. She tried to brush some of the sand from her body but she was so wet it only made her cold fingers sting. Instead, she used the torn fabric to brush over Moonbeam's legs to offer him some relief. She could hear the prince shaking out fabric and presumed he had taken his shirt from around the stallion's head. She knew his skin must be sore from where he'd been pelted by the storm.

'Thank you,' she said stiffly.

'For what?' His deep voice sounded beside her and she jumped because she hadn't heard him move and couldn't see a thing in the blackness.

'For protecting my horse.'

'If he had died, so would we,' he bit out.

Okay, so that cleared up any notions she'd had about him being thoughtful. About to move as far away from him as possible she let out a shriek when he put his hands on her shoulders and worked them down to her waist.

Incensed at the invasion of her person, Farah slapped his hands away. 'I told you I don't have any more weapons.'

'Where's your mobile phone?'

Feeling small and helpless compared to his size and strength, she shoved at his wide chest, thankful that it was now covered in fabric. 'Why would I have a mobile phone when our village doesn't have coverage?'

He cursed and moved away from her. Farah let out a pent-up breath and gave a hollow laugh, her arms coming around her body to ward off the chill. 'Swearing won't help, and you only have yourself to blame, because your father refused to spend money on anyone but himself.'

He ignored the jab and once again she heard the rustle of fabric.

'What are you doing?' she demanded as he pulled Moonbeam's blanket off.

'We need this more than he does.'

'You can't just take it off. He'll freeze.'

'He will not freeze. He has a thick coat of hair and he's mostly dry. We are not.'

As if on cue, another huge shiver wracked her body and she rubbed her arms. The wind howled outside their rocky respite but at least it didn't cut right through her any more. Too tired to argue, she dropped to her knees on the hard ground.

'You're too close to the opening there. Come here.'

How he knew her location was beyond her. 'I'm fine.'

'That wasn't a request,' he growled so close to her she jumped again.

'I'm too tired to argue with you' she snapped. 'Just let me be.'

'The way your father let me be?'

Farah closed her eyes. She didn't want to think about why they were in this predicament because she knew her father had been wrong to do what he'd done, even if he did think his reasoning was solid. 'Did I not just say I was too tired to—hey! Put me down!'

'I too am tired, I'm also hungry and angry, so I would advise you not to test the limits of my patience because that ran out three days ago when your father refused to release me. He hasn't had the courage to face me since.'

'My father is not a coward!'

'No?' He placed her on the ground more gently than she expected, given the roughness of his hold. 'So you condone his actions? Or perhaps you assisted him.' When he sat beside her Farah automatically scooted sideways to get away from him but he grabbed her arm and yanked her back. Then he anchored her with his forearm and pulled her backwards until she was lying on her side with him plastered along her back, his knees pressing into the backs of hers.

'I'm not sleeping with you!'

He tugged the horse blanket over the top of them. 'No, you're not. You're sleeping *next* to me. There's a big difference, *habiba*, and believe me you would not be invited to do the former.'

Farah felt her blood boil at his arrogance.

'But there is only one blanket,' he continued, shifting

her even closer. 'And, given that you can't stop shaking, we need to share body heat to warm up. Relax and this will go a lot easier.'

Relax? Farah couldn't have been more tense if he'd pointed a loaded gun at her head. It had been a long time since she had been physically close to anyone and all this bodily contact was messing with her head. 'This isn't right.'

'But kidnapping your prince is fine.'

'Must you always have the last word?' she grumbled.

'Must you?'

Not wanting to find anything remotely amusing about him, Farah curled herself into a tight ball to try to put distance between them. Self-sufficiency was a prized trait in the harsh desert climate and Farah was proud that, although she was female, she could survive on her own if she had to. She wanted to point this out to the prince but that would involve speaking to him and she'd much rather pretend he wasn't there. She'd much rather pretend she was in her own bed than on the cold, hard ground wrapped in the strong arms of her father's number one enemy.

Finally she fell asleep. Thank Allah. Once her trembling had subsided, she'd squirmed around trying to get comfortable to the point that Zach had needed to place a staying hand on her hip to stop her from rubbing her bottom against his burning erection one more time. It was bad enough he even had one let alone her knowing about it.

Realising that his hand was still gripping her hip, he eased it away. He knew his reaction to her was based on his recent bout of celibacy and little else. Maybe the way danger heightened the senses, as well. Whatever it was, he had no intention of acting on it. He wasn't the type to lose his head over anything and one slender spitfire wouldn't change that.

Sighing, he shifted to get comfortable. The little spitfire whimpered in her sleep like a small kitten having a bad dream. He didn't doubt she was and he wondered if it featured a jail cell and the span of twenty years. That brought a small smile to his lips, one that was quickly supplanted by a scowl when she burrowed closer to his warmth. He briefly thought about putting his arm beneath her head to offer his biceps as a pillow but then dismissed the idea. What did he care about her comfort? She might have offered him food earlier and… Damn. Just the thought of her crouching over him and bringing the food to his lips was enough to have his mind spiralling back to what she would look like naked. He'd noticed the telltale flush of arousal on her face when he'd drawn her fingers into his mouth and laved them with his tongue, the way her eyes had glazed with desire. She'd been turned on and, damn it, so was he. Again.

Absently he wondered if she was intimate with the arrogant soldier who had argued with her. He clearly wanted her. Not that Zach cared, but there was definite tension between the two of them. The man was clearly a moron, though, to have left her alone with him. If she had been his woman there was no way he'd have let her have her own way in a dangerous situation. She would be his to take care of. His to protect. And thank Allah she wasn't.

He felt her shiver and curl into a tighter ball. She must still be cold; he damned well was. Cold, hungry, angry and his arms and torso felt like they were covered in a thousand tiny pinpricks from where the sand and rain had pelted him in the storm.

He let out an aggrieved sigh. Farah Hajjar better not give him any trouble in the morning because he was very far from his cool, controlled self.

CHAPTER FIVE

'WAKE UP, ZENOBIA. Time to hustle.'

Hustle?

Groggily Farah came awake and realised the prod in her bottom had been the Prince of Bakaan's foot. Her teeth ground together at the way he mockingly referred to her as a warrior queen from the Roman era. Some warrior she was, allowing him to get the better of her. 'Only if you'll give me back my dagger so I can do to you what she did to Probus.'

She sat up and rubbed the grit from her eyes but still caught the look of surprise on his face. 'Oh, sorry,' she simpered. 'Am I supposed to play the part of the village idiot who isn't anywhere near as learned as the high and mighty prince with his first-class degree?'

He didn't move but she felt his eyes on her like a hot brand. 'Two degrees, actually.'

'Oh, well, excuse me.' She glanced at Moonbeam so she wouldn't have to look at him.

'So you're educated?'

'Self-educated, no thanks to your family's reign.' She flicked him a scathing look. 'But, as much as your father tried to keep us all in the dark, we're a little more resourceful than you might think. Especially when—'

She stopped, suddenly realising she was about to tell him that there was someone on his staff who was supplying the outer tribes with contraband medical and educational goods.

Great going, Farah, she admonished herself. *What a way to get a man fired—or, worse, killed.*

His eyes narrowed. 'When what?'

She brushed sand off her legs. 'Never mind. Why did you kick me?'

'I didn't kick you. I nudged you.' His deep voice made her insides feel unsteady. 'And I wouldn't be Probus in your little fantasy. I'd be Aurelian.'

Aurelian, who had captured Zenobia and ended her reign as queen. She made a rude noise at his arrogance. 'You wish,' she muttered, half under her breath.

He stopped in front of her and she stared at his dusty boots and the way his jeans—so foreign in her part of the world and yet so sexy in the way they moulded to his legs—hung over the top. 'I captured you, didn't I?'

Instant annoyance hit her at his words and she threw her head back to glare at him—only something black and alive dropped to the ground beside her and she let out a blood-curdling scream. The scorpion took off into a nearby crevice and Farah went from paralysed inertia to violently brushing at her clothing in seconds.

Suddenly large hands grasped her upper arms and lifted her to her feet. 'Keep still.' The prince scoured the ground for the offending visitor and released her. 'It's gone.'

Something crawled across her shoulder and she nearly hit the cave roof. 'More! There's more.'

'No, there's not.' The prince's voice seemed to come from far off before he gripped her arms again and shook her gently. 'It's your imagination.'

'My hair,' she gasped. 'They're in my hair.' It was one of those irrational fears she'd struggled to master since her mother's death all those years ago.

With an exaggerated sigh, the prince gently knocked her hands away from her head and turned her around.

Zach's eyes swept over dark chestnut tresses that a bird would think twice about before nesting in. It was long, thick and matted with sand, half of it still in the braid that hung down her back.

Carefully he scanned it for anything moving. 'There is nothing.'

'There is. I can feel...' She shivered and turned towards him. Her eyes were huge in her face and moist from where she held tears at bay. She was afraid he realised; truly petrified. Something inside his chest pulled tight and before he could question the move he dug his fingers into her hair. She stood stock-still but he caught the small tremors of fear racing through her and the need to comfort her overwhelmed everything else.

Smoothing her hair back from her face, he moved behind her to unwind her plait. The dark waves parted beneath his fingers and he found himself studying the lightly tanned skin of her neck. It looked smooth and supple, not unlike the body he had curved around the night before.

Reminding himself that she was as bloodthirsty as her father, he ignored the underlying silky texture of her hair as he combed his fingers through it. Again his body responded to the fact that he was touching her, which only elevated his already soaring stress levels. He should be focused on getting home, not on saving a woman he couldn't care less about from desert insects.

Roughly he turned her back to face him. 'You're clear.'

She stared up at him with those guileless chocolate-brown eyes and he felt a jolt go right through him. Bedroom eyes, he decided, his gaze automatically dropping to her slightly parted lips. Bedroom eyes and soft, kissable lips...

Time seemed to stop as he imagined doing all sorts of unholy things to those lips, starting with his mouth and ending with... The hair on his forearms stood on end and it wasn't the only thing that did.

Hell.

He stepped back and took himself in hand—metaphorically speaking.

Farah stiffened as the prince moved away and grabbed hold of Moonbeam's halter.

She shook off the lethargy that had invaded her limbs as soon as he had touched her, as soon as he had looked at her mouth—as if it were the ripest peach and he couldn't wait to sink his teeth into it. For a tense moment she had thought he might kiss her, and she was ashamed to admit that she had wanted him to. But how could she when he was the kind of man she had vowed to avoid? A man who walked all over others in order to further his own interests. Not to mention the reason behind the situation they were in. 'He needs water,' she muttered, knowing it must be true because her lips were as dry as the desert itself.

'Water and food,' he agreed shortly. 'But unless you can divine it from these rocks he isn't going to get any here. Nor are we.' He patted the stallion. 'He's an impressive animal. What's his name?'

'Moonbeam.'

The laughter that followed her announcement was both warm and strong. 'You should have just gelded him when you named him. It would have been easier on him.'

'Oh, you're hateful.'

'When I want your opinion, I'll ask for it.' He sobered and threaded his fingers together to form a platform. 'Give me your foot.'

'I'm not coming with you!' He had to be mad to suggest it, the hateful, arrogant—

'Fine.' He straightened and vaulted onto Moonbeam as if the stallion was no bigger than a Shetland.

Hold on. 'What are you doing?'

'Leaving.'

'Not on my horse.' She grabbed onto the halter. He couldn't just leave her here without any way of getting home. 'Damn it, why did you have to come into my life?'

He stared down at her. 'I've been asking myself the same question. Now, get on or I'll leave you to become buzzard food.'

Farah thought about telling him to go to hell but knew that she couldn't. Yet. 'This time I'm riding on the back.' No way was she going to be made to feel small and helpless by having his arms wrapped around her again.

'I don't care if you ride on your head. Just move it.'

Knowing this was probably a mistake, but aware that she really had little option, Farah stomped to his side. He'd wrapped part of her dark tunic around his head again and, even though he was as dusty and as unkempt as she was, he managed to look regal and magnificent atop her snorting stallion. When their eyes connected she refused to let herself be swayed by his looks and injected as much venom into her gaze as she could.

Stony-eyed, he reached out his much larger hand for her to take. As soon as she placed hers in it he yanked her up behind him as if she weighed little more than a pillow.

Unfortunately, riding behind him didn't make her feel any better than riding in front, because she was forced to hold tightly to his lean hips as he urged Moonbeam to get them to safety.

Which came in the form of a nearby tribal village some hours later, just when she thought she might expire. The tribe was a fair distance from her own so she knew they had covered a lot of ground the night before, desperation and adrenaline pushing them on. She didn't know anyone in the village, not having much cause to leave her own, and was surprised when their leader bought the prince's charming 'lost in the storm with one of his servants' scenario.

Servant!

Oh, how she wished she could contradict him but the consequences weren't worth it.

With a promise that Moonbeam would be housed until he could return, the prince ate down a mountain of food before borrowing a battered jeep and driving them through most of the afternoon and night, with only the occasional rest for a power nap. Farah didn't know how he kept up the pace and after a night of little rest, slept most of the way.

Awakening just before dawn her eyes were riveted to the changing landscape and the size of the city of Bakaan as they approached the following morning. She'd visited once or twice as a child but she'd forgotten how large it was—and how busy. Even this early the streets were filled with cars, bicycles, oxen and camels with a mass of people dressed in all styles of clothing filling the pavements. Built into a hillside, the Shomas Palace towered over the city in all its golden glory and Farah secretly admired its opulent beauty as Zach identified himself to the guards and drove through the iron gates.

'What do you intend to do with me?' she asked, proud of the way she managed to keep the tremor out of her voice.

Ignoring her question, he jerked the old car to a stop in front of a set of massive stone steps; heat shimmered off the pale sandstone walls of the palace, turning them white. The courtyard they were in was already a hive of activity with a procession of servants rushing around. Farah returned her gaze to the prince's as he rested his hands on the steering wheel, his lion's eyes scanning her face to the point of discomfort.

She raised her chin as if his perusal was nothing more than an irritant. She was hoping he was going to tell her that, now that he was back home, he was going to let her go. That he was going to let the whole thing drop and forget it had even happened. She knew she'd like to. 'Well?' She stared him down. 'Are you going to tell me or not?'

'Yes, I'm going to tell you.' He smiled but it was grim in his hard, beautiful face. 'I'm going to use you as bait.'

Farah fumed as the prince all but dragged her along opulent hallways and past closed doors, servants and guards bowing one after the other as they proceeded; none of them showing an ounce of shock at seeing their prince pulling a woman along roughly by the arm. If possible the interior of the palace was grander than the exterior and Farah's mind buzzed at the wondrousness of the wide hallways and soaring ceilings stencilled in blue, green and gold fretwork prevalent in the Moorish period, the ancient artworks that were framed under bright lights, and the solid marble floor that shone to a high gloss from the sunshine streaming in through high arched windows.

Realising she was letting herself become awestruck, she dug her heels into the polished floor. 'You can't do this.'

Of course he didn't respond to her outraged cry but stopped before an enormous carved door. Ignoring her, he turned towards two guards who had rushed to follow them. 'No one comes in here, no one goes out—is that clear?'

'Yes, Your Highness,' they said in unison.

'I won't let you use me this way,' Farah asserted as he shoved her into the room.

When he gave a short, sharp laugh she stared at him belligerently. 'You have no grounds to hold me.'

The prince turned cold, menacing eyes on her and for the first time she noticed the deep brown ring that bordered all that gold. 'I don't need a reason.'

'Right. Your word is law, is that it?' Farah tossed her filthy hair which she'd replaited after the prince had sifted his fingers through it back over her shoulder.

He stepped into her space and brought his face level

with hers. 'That is it, yes. An eye for an eye. Isn't that what your father believes in?'

Her father did unfortunately hold to that cynical view of the world but Farah didn't.

Dismissing her, he turned towards a maid she hadn't noticed slip into the room behind them. Only half listening to what he was saying to the girl, Farah took in the scope of the opulent room for the first time. And what she saw made her gasp out loud.

'Oh, my…is this the harem?'

'What gave it away?' the prince drawled lazily. 'The cherub motifs on the wall or the large sunken marble tub in the middle of the room?' He walked over to it and raised his foot to rest on the curved edge like the insolent sheikh that he was.

Farah told herself not to react but it was no good. There was something about him that pushed all reason out of her brain and replaced it with…with something she did not want to identify. 'I'm not staying in here.'

'No?' He raised a brow. 'Admittedly the soft furnishings are quite old but it's about to be renovated. Perhaps the updated version will be more to your liking.'

'I won't be around long enough to see it,' she promised.

'Don't be so sure.' He straightened and headed back to her. His nose twitched. 'See that she has a bath,' he said to the maid, although he didn't take his eyes from hers.

See that she… Farah's gaze narrowed into angry slits. If he thought she would just fall in with his plans he was wrong. There was no way she was going to wait around in this horrible room for her father to show up. If she could somehow escape and get back to him she would.

Her silence must have spoken volumes because he cast her a condescending smile. 'I can almost hear your mind ticking over, and if you're thinking of trying to leave I would advise against it.'

Farah angled her chin up and suddenly their faces were

only inches apart, his gaze fixed on her mouth. It was impossible not to be aware of him, and for one—no, two—erratic heartbeats she thought he was going to kiss her and her breath backed up in her lungs. Then he moved away. Slowly.

Incensed that she had stood there like a besotted idiot instead of pushing him away, she lashed out in a show of rash pride. 'Fortunately for me, I don't have to take your advice.'

He regarded her with a cool look that said he knew exactly what he did to her. 'Just try it and see how far you get.'

Oh, she wanted to. She wanted to do that and more. And the feeling only grew worse when he reached the main door and turned back, his gaze raking her from head to toe and making her tingle with hot, impotent fury.

'And burn those clothes she's wearing,' he instructed the maid. 'There's no soap in the world that will kill that smell.'

Striding from the room, Zach was wondering what the hell he was going to do with the spitting she-cat who was more trouble than she was worth when Staph rushed towards him.

'Highness, I just heard of your return. We were all so worried about you.'

Zach grimaced. He needed to bathe, to burn his own clothing and to find his brother in that order. 'I'm back now.' He set off in the direction of his private wing. 'Where's Nadir?'

'Preparing for his wedding.'

That stopped him in mid-stride. 'His what?'

'His wedding, Your Highness. He is marrying mistress Imogen today.'

Today!

Well that at least explained the extraordinary amount of activity he'd noticed in and around the palace.

Hell. Talk about bad timing.

Forgetting all about a shower for now, he left Staph and trawled the palace for Nadir, eventually finding him holding a small dark-haired infant that could only be Zach's new niece. Gazing into her wide-spaced gray-blue eyes, Zach felt something uncurl inside his chest. How was it that his brother had what he had always wanted for himself, while all he could do was think about bedding some woman who was wholly unsuitable for him? The irony of the situation wasn't lost on him. He thought of the email he'd received from Amy, but it wasn't her face that filled his head—it was Farah Hajjar's.

'Where the hell have you been?' his brother barked at him. 'You have a lot of explaining to do.'

Nadir's curt words brought Zach's attention back to the present. '*I* do?' He raised a dust-covered eyebrow. 'Thanks for the concern and the belated rescue team.'

Nadir frowned. 'You look like hell. What happened?'

Knowing now wasn't the time to go into detail, Zach shrugged. 'The short version is that I had an unfortunate run-in with one of the less welcoming tribes in the mountains.'

'Hell. For a while I thought you were holed up with a woman.'

Zach laughed, a ripple of discomfort running through him as he thought about the feel of Farah's surprisingly strong arms wrapped around his belly as they'd raced across the desert on horseback. It had surprised him how alive he had felt—possibly because he'd been imprisoned for three days—and how connected to the desert he'd felt for a change. He'd been surprisingly connected to those soft little breasts nuzzling against his back, as well. 'I suppose technically you could say that I was, but it wasn't by choice, and she's more like a spitting she-cat than a woman. One who is currently locked in the old harem.'

He grimaced as Nadir's eyebrows shot skywards. 'Not the most convenient situation on your wedding day, but then I didn't know it was your wedding day until a moment ago.'

Nadir stared at him as if he had two heads. 'You have a woman locked in the harem?'

'Farah Hajjar, to be exact,' Zach growled, his words laced with disgust.

'Mohamed Hajjar's daughter!'

'One and the same.'

Nadir swore. 'Hajjar will have your head for that.'

Zach's gaze turned wry. 'They both very nearly did.'

'For the love of…' Nadir's gaze narrowed. 'You didn't compromise her, did you?'

Zach gave a sharp bark of laughter. 'A wild boar couldn't compromise that woman, and nor would it want to.' Which should have been the truth, and would be, now that he was back home and out of danger. 'I take it this is my niece?'

'You're changing the subject.'

'I am.' He smiled at her. 'She's beautiful.'

'I know.' He could see that Nadir wanted to ask him more but then he shook his head. 'I don't have time to get the details now, but you're okay?'

'No thanks to you,' he teased his big brother, as he used to when they were boys.

'Ever heard of the boy who cried wolf?' Nadir arched a brow. 'That will teach you for playing so many tricks as a kid.'

Zach grinned. 'Come chat while I get cleaned up.'

'I can't.'

'Why not? The wedding isn't for hours yet.'

'No, but…' Nadir shook his head, clearly distracted by something. 'Here, take your niece and get acquainted.'

He handed the wide-eyed child to him and Zach took her easily. She immediately gazed up at him and he nestled her close. He caught his brother's expression and grinned. 'Hey, don't look so surprised. I'm okay with babies. They're like women and horses—handle them with the utmost care and don't do anything to rub them up the wrong way. Isn't that right, *habibti*?'

Zach immediately thought about the woman he'd left

in the harem. He hadn't exactly handled her with care but then he hadn't exactly been in the mood to. Then there was the fact she was more street urchin than woman—except for those breasts and that mouth.

'Don't let her cut herself on that, and if she cries take her to Maab.'

Zach smiled down at his niece, who was patting the scruff on his face. Hell, he must smell terrible, as well.

'Where will you be?' he asked, but Nadir had already taken off up a flight of stairs and Zach had a feeling he knew precisely where he was headed. He was about to call out that it was bad luck to see the bride on his wedding day but let it go.

The baby in his arms gurgled and looked a little uncertain now that her father had disappeared but he gave her a reassuring smile. It was true what he'd said, horses and women loved him, and he saw no reason why a baby would be any different. He bounced her gently in his arms and stared into her big eyes. 'So, kid, your parents are getting married?' She stared back and he laughed. 'A big step. Are you happy about it?'

She touched his face again and made a litany of garbled sounds.

'Great. Then I am, too.'

He wandered around with her for a bit longer and then sought out Maab when she started fussing.

'I think she's hungry,' he told the elderly woman.

She smiled and cooed at his niece. Then she wrinkled her nose at him.

'I know, I know.' He backed away, 'I smell like death warmed up.' He could also do with some more food.

Heading back to his private apartment, he organised a light meal to be sent up for after his shower and wondered if the spitfire in the harem was hungry. Then he grimaced. He'd known immediately that Nadir wasn't happy about the situation and neither was he. He really didn't have a firm plan as to what he was going to do with her but involving the local police wasn't something he intended to do on his brother's wedding day.

No, she would just have to wait, and perhaps that would be a good thing. His fight wasn't with her but with her father. He had no doubt the old man would be furious that he'd taken Farah, but if Mohamed was prepared to trade himself for her, Zach would let her go.

An eye for an eye.

That was his father's way, not his, yet he was so damned angry right now he didn't care. Fury replacing rational thought. But then being kidnapped, riding through a sandstorm and driving for nearly twenty-four hours would do that to a man. As would wanting to put his hands all over Mohamed Hajjar's spitfire of a daughter. He wondered if she had already completed her bath. Wondered how she would smell when the stink of camel was cleaned from her body. An X-rated fantasy started playing out in his head. A fantasy that entailed both of them wet and naked while he tasted every delicious inch of her.

By Allah, she wasn't even his type.

He scrubbed a wet hand over his face, twisting the shower nozzle to full-on hot, and soaped the stink from his own body. Maybe he'd find a woman he could spend the night with at the wedding. Doubtful, he knew, since he had no idea whether there would be any European women invited, but maybe he'd get lucky. Maybe there would be someone there who was interested in a night of pleasure and relaxation. And Zach was not being immodest in knowing he could give it to her. He was thirty-two and he enjoyed a healthy libido. A healthy libido he'd unhealthily left unattended for too long if his earlier lust for Farah Hajjar was any indication.

He shut off the shower and shook the water from his

hair. There would be no reason for him to have to see Farah Hajjar again after this so it was time to put her from his mind altogether. Something he was very happy about, he mused as he pulled on a clean robe and turned his mind to his brother's wedding.

Dressed and ready to go, Zach was surprised to find Staph knocking on his door. The old man twisted his hands together, his face marred with concern. Immediately Zach wondered if something had happened to Farah. Had she hurt herself? Had someone hurt her?

'What is it, man?' he snapped, uncharacteristically curt. 'Speak up.'

'It's your brother, Your Highness. He has called off the wedding and asked that I send all the guests home.'

Zach shook his head. So much for relaxing once he got home.

Not wasting any time on niceties when he found Nadir seated behind his father's desk, he strode into the room. 'What are you doing?'

His brother looked up at him and smiled as if there was nothing wrong. Which told Zach that something was drastically wrong. 'Working. You look better.'

'It's amazing what a shower and a shave will do.' Zach parked himself in the chair opposite the desk. 'Why are you working? You're getting married in a few hours.'

His brother tried to stare him down but Zach was a master communicator who had always been sensitive to the nuances of others. He was also doggedly determined to get to the bottom of the problem before Nadir completely closed off and made a hash of everything.

Thirty minutes later he'd managed to talk his brother down from the ledge. 'I know you think you're pretty clever,' Nadir said. 'But frankly I wouldn't wish this sick feeling in my gut on anyone.'

Zach shook his head. 'I would love to care for a woman

as much as you do yours,' Again he thought of Amy Anderson and again Farah's face annoyingly intruded. Frustrated that he didn't seemed to have any control over his thoughts, he gritted his teeth. 'Instead,' he began, forcing a lightness into his tone he didn't feel, 'I have to figure out how to stop myself from being shackled to a living, breathing fire-eater who would as soon run me through with a *kanjhar* than look at me.'

'I doubt her father will push it. He hates our family.'

'It's fine.' Zach waved away Nadir's concern, hoping he'd given his brother the right advice. He could think of nothing worse than a man spilling his guts to a woman only to have her politely reject his advances.

Of course there would be nothing polite about Farah Hajjar's rejection…and why the hell was he still thinking about her? 'I can deal with Farah and her insane old man,' he assured his brother. 'You just do us both a favour and go get your woman.'

'Prince Zachim!' At the sound of Staph's breathless cry and harried appearance in the doorway, Zach frowned. Surely he wasn't about to tell him that the sky had fallen in? 'You need to come quick.' Staph drew in another life-saving breath and Zach thought about reminding him that he was too old to be running around the palace like a man half his age. 'The woman you put in the harem has disappeared.'

Zach immediately stilled. 'Disappeared?' He frowned. 'That's impossible. I've put an experienced guard on the door.'

'Yes, my lord,' Staph panted. 'He can't find her.'

Stunned, Zach let off a list of expletives that would have caused his delicate mother to faint if she'd heard him. Surely a slip of a woman like Farah couldn't have bested him?

His brother made a comment but Zach didn't hear it. Within minutes he had rounded up his most trusted guards and was halfway to the harem.

CHAPTER SIX

FARAH STOPPED INSIDE a shadowed doorway to collect herself and get her bearing amidst the labyrinth of busy city streets and buildings. Initially she'd thought there would be no chance of escaping the arrogant prince but in the end it had been remarkably easy.

A workman's forgotten extension ladder in the garden had provided the necessary equipment for her to scale the high wall, and the preparations for some big celebration at the palace had added the perfect cover. In her freshly laundered *abaya*, Farah had looked like any other servant going about her business, or ending her shift with a bunch of others as they headed out of the palace grounds.

Now, standing on a busy street corner, her only goal was to get as far away from the prince as she could and back to her father. First, though, she had to navigate the hot, noisy, dusty city. Glancing at the position of the sun she decided to head north and started zigzagging her way through the moving sea of bodies around her.

She knew that asking for help wasn't an option. She had a feeling if she tried to hitch a ride from a passing motorist he'd probably take her to the police. And what would she tell them—that the Prince of Bakaan planned to use her as bait to bring her father out to charge him with kidnapping? Not going to happen.

Glancing left and right, Farah hurried down a narrow

walkway with high buildings on either side and found herself in a large, quiet square that gave off a bad vibe. She kept the scarf on her head pulled firmly forward and moved with purpose in case anyone tried to stop her.

'Hot afternoon for a stroll, Miss Hajjar.' That deep, taunting voice she had grown to hate had her swinging round towards a nearby alley. Squinting into the shadows she could just make out the prince's imposing shoulders before he stepped into the sunshine. 'I have to confess I usually prefer to stay indoors when it's this hot.'

Farah's body temperature just grew a little hotter. He'd found her! How was that possible? She was sure no one had noticed her leave and as far as the maid was concerned she was planning to have a sleep. Frustration zinged through her as he leant one shoulder lazily against the sandstone wall of a building, as if they were two friends meeting at a planned rendezvous. But they weren't. They were sworn enemies and this time she was ready for him. This time she would not be caught off guard by the shape of his horrible mouth that looked even more sinfully seductive in his cleanly shaven jaw.

Oh, dear Allah, but he was attractive!

Her lower body clenched alarmingly, her breathing erratic, and she knew it wasn't just from the adrenaline speeding through her body at the presence of danger. It was him. He did things to her, stirred things up inside her, she didn't want to think about.

Pushing that aside, she forced her attention away from her body and back to the tautly honed male that she knew was tensed to strike despite his relaxed stance. He was dressed in a black *dishdasha*, his freshly shaven jaw doing nothing to make him look more civilised than the unshaven version. In fact he looked even more ruggedly handsome, every inch the powerful male in control of his surroundings. He drew her like the devil himself and a frisson of helpless fear went through her as he silently surveyed her.

The feeling made her so angry she drew the sword she gripped tightly in the folds of her dress before she could think better of it. 'If you take another step, you'll regret it,' she warned.

He glanced at her weapon and raised an amused eyebrow. 'Is that so?'

By Allah, his insolence was insulting and she unconsciously shifted into a purely combative stance. She wasn't stupid enough to think that she could win a real contest with him—he dwarfed her in height and breadth—but maybe, just maybe, she could take him by surprise and land him on his backside long enough to dash through the maze of streets that led back to the busy souk. There she could blend with everyone else and disappear in the sheer volume of human bodies.

As far as plans went, it wasn't much of one, but since giving up wasn't an option either she held her ground.

'Did you know,' he drawled, inspecting his fingernails as if every one of his senses wasn't attuned to her slightest movement. 'There are at least twenty-five ways to kill a person with your bare hands?'

No, she hadn't known that. 'Right now, I'd settle for just one.' She held the sword tighter and waited for him to come at her. Instead he threw his head back and laughed.

The sight and sound of his amusement disconcerted her because she'd been serious!

'Put the sword away, Farah,' he instructed softly, all pretence at relaxation over.

Farah's fingers flexed around the hilt. The way he said her name in that rough, sexy voice sent a sharp, sweet ache straight to her pelvis but she ignored it. 'No.'

His eyebrows climbed his forehead. 'I was starting to

think that you were smart, my little Zenobia. Are you about to prove me wrong?'

She had trained with a few of her father's respected bodyguards before he had put a stop to it. They'd soon see who wasn't very smart. 'I escaped, didn't I?' she taunted.

A muscle ticked in his jaw. Good. An angry man made more mistakes than a rational one.

'My guards found you.' His eyes fell to the glint of the sun shining off the sharp blade of her rapier.

Farah curled her lip. 'Your guards are incompetent. I doubt they could find a particle of dust in a sandstorm. Perhaps they are poorly trained.'

The muscle flickered again in his jaw and a small smile threatened to curve her lips at how easily she got to him. He'd been lucky when he'd grabbed her at her father's camp. He wouldn't be so lucky this time.

'It's not a good idea to prod an angry lion,' he drawled as he pushed away from the wall. 'They tend to bite.'

A shiver snaked down Farah's spine at the warning implicit in that drawl; his voice was deep and melodious, as if he were paying her a grand compliment. 'I think you got lucky coming upon me now,' she challenged. 'If your men had truly found me, why didn't they take me?'

'They were ordered not to.'

'Why?' Farah tensed as he took another step toward her, the overhead sun highlighting his chiselled features.

The square behind her was deathly quiet but she didn't take her eyes off the prince to find out why. Nothing was more dangerous to her right now than this man. She raised her sword in preparation to strike, sweat making her palms slippery. 'Were you afraid they'd get hurt?'

'No.' He circled to her right and she pivoted on her slippered feet to follow him. 'I was afraid you would.'

His black robes billowed as he prowled around her and

she knew beneath the soft trousers his strong thighs would be tensed to spring at her.

'Put the sword down. You won't win this battle.'

Farah didn't say anything but her keen eyes caught movement on the rooftop above him so she knew that they weren't alone. She let her lip curl into an insolent sneer. 'Need help to bring in one woman, Prince Zachim?'

'Oh, I think I've already proven that I don't need help bringing you in, little cat.'

'Ha!' She was scornful. 'You got lucky the first time. You caught me by surprise.'

'Really?' His teeth sank into his fleshy bottom lip as his gaze dropped to her mouth, telling her more than words that he knew exactly what had distracted her the first time. 'Who's to say it won't happen again?'

'Me,' she snapped, humiliated by her own weakness where he was concerned. Why, oh, why did her body find his so damned fascinating? It made no sense at all.

The cumbersome *abaya* dragged around her legs as she shifted to keep him in sight. If she got the chance she was going to have to toss modesty to the wind and lift her skirts to try and outrun him. 'I know you have a sword on you.' She lifted her chin. 'Draw it or get out of my way.'

'I'm not going to fight you.'

'Afraid?' she challenged.

He smiled. 'Give it up. We both know you have no chance of beating me.'

Farah stilled. His voice was so controlled, so knowing. He was calling her bluff, damn him, and a deep desire to do the opposite, a deep desire to *show* him, turned her muscles hard. For a brief moment she indulged in the reckless fantasy of besting him, of being the one to bring the mighty Prince of Bakaan and his monumental ego to his knees. Could she do it?

'I can take you,' she said, twisting the sword in a few

expert loops, testing it for weight and balance. It wasn't a great piece of craftsmanship but it was better than nothing.

A slow smile spread across his face. 'Now, that I'd like to see.'

Oh! She caught the not so subtle innuendo in his tone and lunged at him, hoping to catch him off guard, realising too late that that was exactly what he'd wanted her to do.

Moving with impressive speed for a man his size, he dodged her blade and she heard the hiss of metal against leather as he unsheathed his own. Adrenaline raced through her veins and charged her body. This was what she needed—a good bout of sparring to rid her of all the tension, fear and worry that threatened to swallow her whole.

She charged him again and brought her sword crashing down against his as hard as she could. She didn't let up and the clash of steel was the only sound ringing in the small empty square around them. Although, as to that, a thousand spectators could have been watching and she wouldn't have noticed.

The adrenaline seemed to give her added strength, but even so she couldn't detect any weakness in him that would give her an advantage.

'Cease this, Farah,' he ordered, using his sleeve to wipe the sweat from his brow.

Distracted by the sight of his muscular forearm it was she who was caught off guard when his sword unexpectedly came down over hers with so much force her teeth rattled.

It was as if he'd only been using half his strength before, and irritation that he would go easy on her gave her a burst of energy and she rushed him, both exhilarated and appalled when she heard the rip of fabric.

Absolute shock held them both immobile and, horrified, Farah watched as bright red blood bloomed from the dark sleeve of his robe.

Oh, dear Allah... She hadn't really meant to hurt him...
Her appalled gaze rose to his. Instinct finally kicked in at
his ferocious expression and she dropped the sword before
taking off towards a nearby alley.

Sweat and fear made her more clumsy than usual and
she screamed when she felt a hand grab hold of her head-
scarf. Fortunately the fabric gave and Farah shot into the
alleyway.

The pounding of his footsteps behind her alerted her as
to how close he was right before his arm reached around
her and yanked her back against him.

Incited by real terror, Farah fought him with all her
might but it seemed to take him only seconds to subdue
her and have her pinned face first against a rough wooden
door, her hands stretched above her head and his hip angled sideways as he forced her legs apart to hold her lower
body still.

Completely powerless, Farah leaned her hot face against
the rough cool wood and listened to her heart hammering
inside her chest.

Zach steadied his uneven breathing as he held the little
wild cat hard against the door, his eyes shifting to the cut
on his arm. It stung but he knew it wasn't deep because
he'd felt her pull back at the last second. Really he should
have disarmed her straight away but he'd been enjoying
sparring with her too much. She was good—no match for
his strength, but she was nimble and he'd felt that same
exhilarating spark he had felt riding with her in the desert. It had been a long time since he'd felt this energised,
this *alive*, and he wondered how much of it was the sense
of danger or the woman before him.

As if sensing his distracted thoughts, she suddenly
bucked against him to try and dislodge him and Zach
pressed her harder against the wood. It occurred to him

that she might have more weapons on her and that he'd need to pat her down before he released her. The thought brought an image of his hands drifting over her lithe body, shedding her of her clothes as he went, and he hardened in anticipation. He cursed silently. For some reason her body acted like a lure for his and he was fast running out of plausible explanations to justify it. As far as sex went, he usually had to like a woman to want her.

He eased back slightly and barely fought the urge to shift his stance so that his erection could nestle against her rounded backside. By Allah, that would feel good, soft and warm, and if he bent his knees a little he could push himself against the apex of her thighs. With his attention so acutely consumed by her femininity, he thickened even more, aching with a need he was hard-pressed to remember feeling before.

He unconsciously breathed in her sweet scent from the oils used in her bath and he felt a sharp sting against his shin for his efforts. The little wild cat had kicked him and even managed to get a hand free as his hold had unconsciously slackened. By Allah, he needed to get a grip.

Restraining her once more, he leaned in close. 'You would have done better if you'd used that agile little body against me for pleasure, Farah, rather than trying to fight me,' he goaded.

Cocoa-brown eyes rounded, sparking with a mixture of fear and anger. And something else. *Hunger? Need?* He drew in a sharp breath. What would she do if he just said to hell with it and kissed her until she was moaning in submission as he'd wanted to do earlier in the harem, moaning for him to take her and pleasure her as no man ever had before?

'I would rather boil myself in oil than try and entice you,' she spat.

Normally Zach had no trouble controlling his libido—

his *emotions*—but this woman could incite a monk to forget his vows. 'Liar,' he said against her skin. He wanted to turn her so that he could feel her curved into him and before he could think of all the reasons why that wasn't a good idea he had her in his arms and his mouth slanted over hers.

He kissed her hard and mercilessly and he didn't stop when she hissed a noise against his lips and thumped his shoulders. He didn't stop as she squirmed to get away from him and he didn't stop when the voice of reason rang out a warning inside his head.

This thing between them had started the minute she'd put those slender fingers in his mouth, maybe even before, and he was uncaring that this was something he would normally never do—uncaring about anything but having her surrender to him. Of having her wind those long legs around his hips so he could satisfy the primal need that owned him and made him want to own her.

When she moaned as if he was hurting her, it penetrated the fog of surging testosterone and he raised his head to look down at her. Her cheeks were flushed bright pink and strands of her silky hair clung to her neck. Her eyes looked too large for her face and her lips were moist and swollen from where he had ravished them. She looked wild and wanton and with every panting breath she took her breasts rose temptingly against his chest.

Shaken by the strength of his reaction to her, Zach thought about releasing her right up until the moment her pink tongue stole out of her mouth and swiped his taste from her lips. It was then he realised she was no longer struggling against him and that her eyes were trained on his mouth in a way that said she wanted more. And, by Allah, so did he.

With a pained groan he lowered his head and once more touched his lips to hers, only gently this time. He wanted to take his time to savour her lips, to feel their texture and taste their unique flavour. He wanted to feel her meet him halfway and he made a guttural sound deep in his chest when she tentatively rose against him in an innocent quest for more. Zach couldn't remember a kiss ever feeling so intimate, so good, and he fell against her, pressing her back into the door.

Thick lashes came down to shield her eyes as if the sensation was too much to bear, as if she could only focus on one thing at a time. He felt her lips give beneath his own, opening wider as he took the kiss deeper, the sensations shaking him to his core. Without even knowing it, he released her hands and wound his through her lush hair, cradling the back of her skull as he positioned her to take his tongue.

He growled as she melted against him, her tongue gliding shyly against his, and his world shrank to encompass only this. Only her. He pulled her in tighter, hitching her higher. She gave a soft, feminine whimper, her fingers clenching at his shoulders as she quivered against him. Zach cursed the amount of clothing between them, unable to stop himself from grinding his erection against the juncture of her thighs. He swallowed the catch in her breath and chased her tongue into her mouth, his hands restless in her hair, restless on her body, as he sought to pull the blasted *abaya* up and over her head so he could get to her body.

Dimly he became aware that they weren't alone. A couple of his senior officers had gathered at the entrance to the alleyway to ensure his safety and were at this moment watching him make love to his little prisoner. It wasn't the best behaviour he'd ever modelled and it took every ounce of willpower he had to let her go and step back from her.

When he did she slumped against the doorway, her eyes

wide, her lips swollen and wet. She looked beautiful. Wild and untamed and just as shocked as he was.

It was the shock that finally brought him to his senses. 'What the hell was that?'

A surfeit of emotions charged across her face, wounded pride being one of them. 'That was you being a bully,' she accused hotly.

Zach felt as if he'd been slapped. His father had been a bully; he wasn't, and as for forcing her, her body had been primed for his kiss from the moment they met. 'You wanted everything you just got,' he snarled. 'And if you try to tell me otherwise I'll strip you naked and prove you wrong.'

'Oh!'

Zach placed a hand on her shoulder and turned her to precede him. 'Consider yourself warned.'

Oh? *Oh?* That was all she could come up with after he'd kissed her into a stupor and then insulted her?

Oh?

By Allah, she could come up with a hundred responses now and if he were here she'd give him every last one of them.

Pacing the lavish harem she'd been locked back up in, with two guards posted *inside* the room, she spun around when she heard the lock turning in the door.

She eyed Prince Zachim with open hostility as he stood in the doorway, flanked on either side by the two maids she'd sent away earlier.

'I see your arm is still attached to your body,' she said, still feeling a little guilty at having hurt him, even though he had completely deserved it. 'What a pity.'

'Yes. No thanks to you.' He stepped into the room, his two lackeys shuffling to keep up. 'I believe I left specific instructions for you to dress.'

She felt her body tense as she took in his wide-legged stance. He was no longer wearing the black robes that had made him look like a menacing pirate earlier, but now wore a regal white one, the colour emphasising his swarthy skin and the deep amber tones of his eyes.

By all that was holy, she still couldn't believe the way she had responded to his kisses back in the alley, and her fingers curled into her palms in an attempt to stave off the memory.

She'd never been kissed like that before. Certainly Amir had never tried to kiss her. In fact she'd only ever been kissed once before, by a youth from a neighbouring country who hadn't had the sense to be afraid of her father. It had been rushed and impossibly chaste compared to the Prince of Bakaan's kisses, which she was not going to think about any more.

'I am dressed,' she said, knowing that he was referring to the purple silk gown that had been brought to her earlier and which she hadn't touched.

His lips quirked. 'So you are. Unfortunately your current outfit will not work for my brother's wedding.'

'What do I care about your brother's wedding?'

'Nothing. Obviously. But I find myself uncomfortable with the notion of leaving you alone again.'

Farah crossed her arms over chest. 'Am I supposed to feel sorry about that?'

'No, my bloodthirsty little heathen, but given your recent behaviour I have no wish to be sitting at my brother's wedding, wondering what plans you're hatching down here in my absence.'

Farah tried not to be pleased at causing him some measure of discomfort. 'Just leave me with your guards. I'm sure we can find some way to occupy ourselves.'

'No doubt,' he murmured. 'But I have no wish to have to discipline any more of my men.'

'Am I really so dangerous, Prince Zachim?'

His mouth kicked up into that crooked grin that made her heart trip just a little. 'More like troublesome.'

'My father won't take the bait, you know,' she asserted, hoping that it was true.

'We'll see.'

Farah gnashed her teeth together at his cavalier attitude. He was so cool as to appear almost bored, but why wouldn't he be? It wasn't his life hanging in the balance.

'In the meantime, Isla and Carine are here to prepare you to be my guest at the wedding.'

Farah's eyes cut to both the women and for the first time she noticed that they were carrying towels and drawstring bags that held goodness knew what.

'And you will cooperate this time.'

The prince's insolent drawl brought her eyes back to his. He looked hard and unyielding, as if she had no choice in the matter. 'There is no—'

'Way you're going to attend?' He flicked his hand in her direction as if she were an irritating insect. 'Yes, I know.' He walked towards her and raised his hand to stay the women, who immediately obeyed. Farah's eyes narrowed and she forced herself to remain rigid as he took the last two steps into her personal space. 'But you will. And you will behave.'

As she was about to tell him to go to hell, he shook his head slowly. 'I can of course just lock you in a cell. Or perhaps it would be better to chain you to your bed. I'd hate you to be uncomfortable.'

The air between them grew thicker, making it harder for her to breathe, and Farah automatically stepped back from him. 'It would be better than having to endure your company for the night.'

She heard one of the women gasp. The prince's eyes

narrowed. 'But who said anything about you being alone in that big *harem* bed?'

A dark, thrilling desire rose up inside of Farah as her head filled with all sorts of debasing images of her shackled to a bed with the prince gloriously naked and aroused in front of her. On top of her. *Inside* of her. Because he would be glorious naked; he would be... Farah clamped down on the thoughts running amok inside her head and tried to think straight.

'What if I apologise on behalf of my father?' she gushed, finally prepared to humiliate herself and bow and scrape for this man if it meant she could get her father out of trouble and her life back to normal. 'What if I make up for what he did in some way?'

He leaned back against the cabinet behind him, his fingers tapping a lazy beat against the curved wood. 'What did you have in mind, *habiba*?'

Farah glanced at the maids. 'I could work for you. I could cook or clean or—'

'I already have enough staff in my employ.'

She bit her lip. 'I could...' She wracked her brain to come up with something else. Surely there was something? 'I could train your horses. Your camels.'

'The palace no longer keeps camels and my horses are well taken care of.'

'Damn it, surely there is something you need?'

His gaze ran over her body, lighting a fiery path as it went. 'Keep going, I'm sure you'll hit on something mutually agreeable at some point.'

Farah frowned. Did he mean...?

You wanted everything you just got...and if you try to tell me otherwise I'll strip you naked and prove you wrong.

Farah's face flamed hotly as his words in the alleyway came back to her. 'Not that!' she cried. '*Never* that!'

'Then we have nothing to discuss,' he said in a bored tone.

'You are every bit the tyrant your father was,' she accused, turning away from him.

Embarrassment and despair swamped her. If she had been a man, this whole situation would never have happened. She would have been by her father's side when he'd come upon the prince's SUV and been able to talk sense into him. And she certainly would never have given into this man's challenge and tried to feed him. What had she been thinking?

About his mouth, a little voice reminded her. *You were thinking about his dreamy mouth.*

Self-disgusted, she was about to stalk over to her bedroom when the prince grabbed her and swung her back to face him, his fingertips digging into her upper arms.

'Dammit, you know how to push my buttons but your father took me hostage for three days before I escaped. If you think that will go unpunished, you're sadly mistaken.' He glowered down at her. 'Now get dressed. And if you cause either of these women another problem you won't find me so lenient next time.'

Farah swallowed hard, determined to show zero emotion in the face of his fury, while inside her whole being was quaking. Watching him stride from the room she waited for the resounding echo from the slammed door to pass before she turned to the two wide-eyed maids, who had probably never said a cross word to the prince in their lives. 'I will bathe myself, is that understood?'

'Yes, my lady.'

CHAPTER SEVEN

'STOP FIDGETING,' the prince whispered out of the side of his mouth for about the fifth time.

Farah dropped her hands to her side once more and pretended to focus on the gorgeous wedding ceremony taking place in front of her. 'This dress doesn't fit,' she complained under her breath.

'It's perfect,' he growled.

It wasn't perfect. It was tight across the bodice, the slender straps exposing her arms and upper chest. The stiletto-heeled shoes she'd been given to wear were also surely torture devices with the way they made her feet ache. In the magazines they had always looked so glamorous and beautiful. On the feet they felt like pincers.

'And smile.'

Tired of his instructions—'no sneering, no balled fists and no attacking anyone at the wedding'—Farah pinned a wide smile to her lips. 'Like this?'

The prince's Adam's apple bobbed as he looked at her. 'Better,' he mumbled, followed by something that sounded like, 'I'd hate to experience the real thing,' before turning back to the proceedings.

Farah surreptitiously studied him in his royal white robes and headdress. He was so virile and masculine and so utterly charming when he wanted to be that she almost believed he was as nice as he seemed.

Except that he'd been grouchy towards her ever since he'd picked her up from the harem and she had no idea what she'd done to prompt his ire again other than exist. Earlier, after he'd stormed out, she had done everything that had been asked of her, intending to lull him into thinking that she would cooperate from now on. She'd let the women apply her make-up, dress her and brush her hair until it gleamed, pinning it up at the front and letting it fall down around her shoulders. When she'd finally looked in the mirror she had barely recognised herself. In fact, she'd thought she looked quite pretty until the prince had taken one all-encompassing glance at her and scowled—just like her father had, over her boots! She didn't know why the prince's bad opinion of her affected her so much but it did and the realisation had set her on edge all over again.

She wondered if he believed her when she'd agreed to the truce he'd requested before marching her from the harem and decided that it didn't matter right now. His brother was in the middle of marrying a Western woman so lovely that Farah had no wish to spoil things. There was just something so utterly romantic about the way Sheikh Nadir gazed at his bride that was totally riveting for Farah.

What would it be like to have a man look at her that way?

Debilitating, a little voice reminded her. It would place her in a life of servitude where her wishes would be overlooked or overruled. It certainly wouldn't make her happy.

She shifted her weight into her heels to relieve the pressure on the balls of her feet and felt Prince Zachim tense. Given his importance in the ceremony, they were standing at the front of the glamorously packed ballroom that was overflowing with white and pastel-pink flowers and deep-green foliage with softly lit candles on every available surface.

She had felt the imprint of a thousand curious eyes on

her as she had made her way slowly to the front of the guests but she hadn't recognised a single face who could help her.

A loud cheer went up in the crowd and Farah realised that the ceremony was over, the glowing couple smiling brightly, the groom totally besotted as he took their daughter from a male guest who hadn't stopped beaming the whole time.

Moving slowly, they stopped in front of Farah and the prince, accepting their congratulations. When the little girl reached out and patted Prince Zachim's jaw, he laughed and murmured to her tenderly, leaning forward to kiss her cheek. Farah was so surprised by the action her whole body went still. He really was the most confounding man, she thought a touch tetchily—one minute hard and ruthless and the next charming and…devastatingly male. Confused and feeling too many emotions at once, she was glad when they hung back and let the procession of guests precede them from the stately room.

Testing her weight on her toes, Farah gingerly stepped forward, trying not to feel as though she was walking on stilts.

'Take smaller steps,' the prince advised roughly.

Farah's head came up. 'Smaller steps?' She stared at him. 'Have you seen the things on my feet?'

Yes, he had, and they were beautiful. She was beautiful, standing there scowling at him, and he wondered how a woman who had never genuinely smiled at him, who had never been anything but defiant in his presence, managed to drive him half-crazy to the point that, even now, he was contemplating taking her to bed regardless of who she was or who he was.

Would she be amenable to the idea? No, not likely, but he knew she'd been as lost in their interlude in the alleyway as he had been, and it probably wouldn't take much effort to return her to that state of stupefied, delirious lust. It sure as hell wouldn't take him long.

He saw a flash of vulnerability cross her delicate features as he continued to eat her up with his eyes and he realised she was nervous. A pang different from lust went through him.

'These are not shoes,' she said indignantly, raising the hem of her gown to reveal delicate stiletto sandals designed with lingerie and sex in mind. 'I have no idea why women wear them.'

Zach swallowed heavily but it did nothing to dislodge the gravel from his voice. 'They elongate the leg and highlight a woman's calves.' And she had sensational legs that went on forever. A sheen of sweat rose up along his hairline. *Absolutely sensational.*

She scowled. 'I think they are meant to control women. Next you'll ask me to darn your socks.'

'I throw away my holey socks.'

'Rich *and* wasteful. It figures.'

She lifted her nose at him and he ground his teeth. 'That's some opinion you have of me, sweetheart.'

'Are you saying I'm wrong?'

'Yes, you're wrong.' She sniffed as if he was a servant who had just offered her substandard fare. 'And not only that but you're prejudiced.'

That snapped her out of her holier-than-though repose. 'I am not,' she declared hotly.

The scent of jasmine and honey entwined together and invaded his senses: his favourite. He sighed, not wanting to fight with her. 'Take my arm.'

She cocked an eyebrow. 'Where would you like me to take it?' she asked sweetly. 'The garbage?'

He bit back a laugh and noticed her own lips twitching. So she had a sense of humour. Who knew? 'As long as you don't take a sharp object to it again, you can take it wherever you like.'

Surprise showed on her face at his rejoinder and then she laughed, a dead sexy, full-on, throaty chuckle he thought he could listen to forever.

Finally she stopped and he lifted his gaze to hers. 'You can lean your weight on me until you get used to the heels,' he offered gruffly.

She hesitated before releasing a long breath and reluctantly placed her hand on his arm as if she were touching dynamite.

Zach lifted her hand off his forearm and placed it in the crook of his elbow. When he felt her fingers curl into the fabric of his robe and cling, he felt as if a heavy object had been placed on his chest. He rubbed it but the sensation remained. So did the memory of the way she had fit in his arms earlier; the heat of her response to his kisses.

He swore under his breath and she glanced at him from beneath kohl-rimmed eyes, her long hair falling forward over one shoulder. Whether she was dressed to the nines as she was now, or wearing combat trousers and an old tunic with her hair matted against her head, she was more beautiful than any woman he'd ever seen in his life. Which couldn't be right. Surely Amy's classically cool beauty had touched him more than Farah's exotic dark looks?

He knew bedding the woman at his side would probably put an end to the hunger he felt for her but that wasn't an option. She was the daughter of his enemy and wanting it to be otherwise was just a fool's errand.

'Why are you looking at me like that?'

The words could have come from a petulant teenager to a parent and he shook his head. 'Because I didn't expect to find you so beautiful.'

A pink flush rose along her cheekbones and she dampened her lips. By Allah...

'You're just saying that to try and lull me so that I won't try to escape again,' she said.

No, he hadn't been, he thought grimly, but now he knew that she intended to do so—even though he had trusted her when she'd agreed to cooperate with him earlier—and he felt like an idiot. 'You know that gold sash draped so artfully around your waist?' he asked.

She raised her pointy little chin at him. 'What of it?'

He leant in so close her scent filled him. 'You take one step in the wrong direction tonight and I'll wrap it around your elegant throat and use it as a leash.'

Oh! Farah felt like screaming. One minute she was enjoying his company and the next she hated him again. But his comment had been a good reminder that she was not, in fact, his guest at this wedding, but his prisoner, and she had her own agenda: escape!

Smiling dutifully at the little group they had joined, she watched the covetous glances the women—the very *married* women—gave the prince. Instinct no doubt told them that the reason he was so completely at ease in his own skin was because he was a man who had known pleasure—and had given it.

A hot flush swept up her neck and she raised her hand to mask it. What she wouldn't give to be back in her little hut and arguing with her father about why she didn't want to get married. It seemed so much more simple than parading around with a man who disturbed her on so many levels.

'I said stop fidgeting.' He cupped her elbow as he directed her away from the avid faces of their small group. 'How are your feet?'

'Hobbled. Yours?'

He chuckled. 'You're delightful.'

She scowled. 'I'm not trying to be.'

'I know. Dance with me.'

Not expecting that request, she wasn't ready when he slid a hand to her lower back, his gaze hot on hers when she glanced up at him. 'I don't dance.'

He considered her for a long moment. 'Don't or can't?' he asked shrewdly.

Farah felt another flush heat her cheeks. 'I...' she began, only to stop as he cast her a crooked grin.

'Can't, then,' he concluded, turning her towards him. 'Don't look so outraged, *habiba*, I will teach you.'

A shiver went through Farah as he moved in closer, his warmth hitting her like a wall. Then his spicy scent made her head foggy. This was so not a good idea. Especially when he was right: she couldn't dance. She'd never thought about learning before, preferring to watch from the sidelines. She hadn't thought about sex much, either, but since meeting the prince it was the single most dominating thought that occupied her time. If he'd been an ordinary man in her village or a neighbouring one, who was considerate of her needs, she might have thought about exploring the chemistry that made her stomach flutter and her insides feel liquid, but he was Zachim, Prince of Bakaan, and he was cut from the same controlling cloth as their fathers.

'Not interested,' she said, trying to ignore the little voice in her head that said dancing with him would be fun. Riding Moonbeam full pelt through the desert was fun. Sitting by the fireside dreaming up impossible adventures with her friends was fun. Dancing with Prince Zachim would not be fun. It would be out-and-out dangerous.

As if reading her mind, he gave her a devastating half smile. 'Come on. You know you want to.'

And there was that innate arrogance of his popping up at the right moment to remind her why she disliked him so much. 'No.'

'Just follow my lead.'

His grin widened as she flashed him a look. 'Do you even understand the word *no*?'

'You never know, Farah, you might enjoy it.'

And wasn't that half the problem? She knew that maybe she would enjoy it. Too much.

Before she could rally her defences against him, he raised his left hand. 'Right hand in mine.'

Farah froze so he reached down and clasped her hand in his. 'Now, left hand on my shoulder.'

Again she froze and again he took control and did it for her.

'Now what?' she asked, her whole body taut as she tried to remain impervious to this nearness.

'Now I put my hand here.' He placed his left hand lightly against her hip and Farah's spine lengthened as she registered the heat of his touch.

Her lips felt dry and she mashed them together. He watched her like a hawk zeroing in on its prey. 'And now?'

'Now we move together.' He smiled, clearly amused by her stoicism. 'It's called a waltz. When I lead with my right leg, you move your left leg back. No, not like that—smaller steps, remember, and slower. My leg is supposed to slide against yours so that it looks like we're moving as one.'

A lone sitar player filled the dance floor with a gentle, teasing ballad and Farah desperately focused on the music as the prince's muscular body lightly brushed her own.

'Close your eyes.'

Her eyes flew to his and she moved her face back when she realised how close they were. 'Why? What are you going to do to me?'

'Nothing you don't want me to.'

Time seemed to grind to a halt as those gravelly words grazed along her nerve endings. She felt her pulse race. Those blasted magazine images wove into her consciousness and heat made her dizzy. Then she realised she was holding her breath and let it out.

'Closing your eyes might help you feel the music,' he suggested, watching her closely.

It might help her forget about how devastatingly handsome he was as well, so she did. On some level it made her awareness of him even more intense, but on another it did help, and before she knew it she could feel herself moving much more gracefully than she would have thought possible.

'You're a quick study,' he murmured against her ear. 'How are the feet now?'

Farah shivered and opened her eyes. She'd forgotten all about her feet but now she could feel the balls of them throbbing. 'Not great.'

He pulled her indecently close. 'Lean against me,' he said roughly.

She wanted to say no, she wanted to move away, but gremlins had invaded her body and suddenly her lids drooped closed and she entered some dreamy realm where her body took over. She wouldn't have said exactly that she was dancing because they were barely moving but it felt lovely. She could feel him against her, hard and so solid. His body was so different from her own and it amazed her how they fit together—as if they were made for each other.

When the music changed tempo her eyes drifted opened and she was embarrassed by how lost she had been in the moment. Her heart beat double time and she was shocked to realise how aroused she was just by dancing with him.

It used to be that her body was more like a machine that did her bidding: arms, legs, hands, feet. Now she was aware of useless things, like her breasts, the hollow space between her thighs, the prince's hand on her hip and a tingling weakness at the back of her knees. Sensations that made her feel fragile and defenceless. And then she wondered if it was the same for him. Did men feel weak and defenceless when lust overtook them? Did Prince Zachim feel that right now, for her? It seemed impossible and yet more shocking was how much she wanted him to want her—she, a village girl, with all the sophistication of a desert mouse. Why, he must have had the most sophisticated lovers in the world. Women like the ones that peppered the wedding and gazed at him with a deep longing. A deep longing Farah never wanted to feel for anyone.

Suddenly feeling claustrophobic, she surprised them both by pulling out of his arms. Wanting Prince Zachim was a betrayal to her father and to everything she wanted for herself: self-sufficiency, independence. *Self-respect.* 'I need to use the bathroom,' she said, furious all over again.

'I'll take you.'

Of course he would, and it was a welcome reminder that she wasn't really a wedding guest but a captive. And she no longer cared about his threats if she tried to escape.

Inside the bathroom there were no windows or back doors so she finished up quickly and returned to the ballroom with him, alert now to where the guards were.

A few men dressed in Western attire came over and talked to the prince and he turned to engage in conversation. Farah half listened and smiled politely, as if she were part of the group when she wasn't. She noticed a small knot of women standing close by and realised they were the partners of the men talking and she was the only woman in this group—a lone gazelle in a pride of male lions.

She didn't bother getting the prince's permission before making her way over to them. Let him stop her if he dared. It wasn't for her to decide how long the leash was and, although earlier she had not doubted he'd tie her dress cord around her neck as punishment for defying him, she knew now that he wouldn't jeopardise his brother's wedding by causing a scene. He wasn't *that* uncivilised.

When one of the women she was only half listening to complained she was hot, Farah could have hugged her.

Taking charge, she suggested they walk on the terrace. Lush gardenias and roses scented the warm evening air but Farah was only interested in where the exit points were.

Cursing the torture devices on her feet, she realised she would have to leave them behind, Cinderella-like, if she got a chance to escape. Only she would be leaving both behind and she didn't want the prince to come after her. Ever.

Making her apologies to the women, she quickstepped down the stone steps as if she knew exactly where she was going and skirted the plethora of plants in the verdant garden. Clearly water restrictions did not apply inside the palace—another black mark against the Darkhan family.

A large stone wall covered in a passion-fruit vine loomed in front of her and she paused to get her bearings.

'The gate is about fifty metres to your left,' the prince drawled from behind her.

Farah groaned softly and expelled all the air in her body. 'I got hot.'

'Really?' His eyebrow rose. 'And I thought that was only while we were dancing.'

Oh! 'A simple enough mistake to make for a man with your sized ego.' She smiled sweetly, giving up all pretence of cooperating with him. What did it matter? He wouldn't let her get away from him now.

His eyes gleamed, no doubt taking her response as some sort of challenge. 'You had goose bumps.'

She hated that ring of confidence in his voice. 'Maybe I was cold,' she retorted.

He grinned. 'Now, we both know that's not true.'

His suggestive tone grated along every one of her nerve endings. 'Oh, to be so sure of yourself.'

'You know,' he began conversationally. 'I almost want

you to make a run for it so that I can use that cord on you after all.'

Farah's hand strayed to her neck. 'You wouldn't dare.'

'Oh, I'd dare, Miss Hajjar. Remember, I'm a barbarian prince.'

'Your brother—'

'Is about to leave with his new wife.'

Farah swallowed. He moved in closer and the urge to take flight warred with a deep-seated determination to stand her ground.

'Your skin looks almost luminescent in the moonlight.' He reached out and stroked his hand down the side of her face. Farah reeled back and would have scratched herself on the vine if the prince hadn't grabbed her elbow. 'Careful, you could hurt yourself.'

Only by giving into the pull of attraction between them, she thought wildly, her heart racing as she fought to maintain control over her senses. 'I'll take my chances with a spiky plant any time,' she threw at him.

Ignoring her smart comment, he drew her inexplicably closer. 'You don't like being told what to do, do you?'

Sensation zipped through her as his hands dropped to her hips and splayed wide. 'Not by men like you, I don't,' she bit out scathingly. Anything to put him off.

'Men like me?' His eyes narrowed dangerously. Soft music and the tinkling conversation from the ballroom drifted over them. 'You need taming, my little Zenobia,' he whispered, taking full advantage of the tilt of her chin to nuzzle his way down her throat. 'And I'm the man to do it.'

The hands she intended to shove against his shoulders slipped and she nearly groaned as her fingers slid along the top of his robe and grazed the ends of his thick hair.

A fierce expression crossed his shadowed face and one of his own hands cupped the nape of her neck, holding her firm. It seemed like forever that they stared at each other, silent and intense, the only sound that of their harsh, un-even breaths and the pounding of her heartbeat she was sure he could hear as loudly as she could.

She felt his hand sift through her hair before he slowly wound its length around his fist. She could feel the tug of each loop at her scalp and she couldn't tear her eyes from his.

'Tell me you want me, Farah.'

His lips slid along her jaw, feather-soft, as he breathed her in. Farah's head fell to the side, unconsciously offering more of her neck to his sinful lips, offering more of herself.

He was going to kiss her. She knew it and she wanted him to. She wanted to feel the moist thrust of his tongue again and lose herself in his dark taste. She wanted him to crush her against him and ease the unbearable ache that throbbed low in her body. Just imagining it had her knees giving out. He took her weight effortlessly, his free hand skimming up the sides of her torso, stealing her thoughts like a sexy cutpurse filching goods from an unprotected market stall. Then, ever so slowly, he brought his other hand down and skated his thumbs lightly along the un-derside of her breasts until her throbbing nipples were so tight they ached for his touch. Ached for his...

'I wouldn't go there if I were you, Zach.'

Shocked and dazed by the voice at her side, Farah whipped her head around to find Sheikh Nadir scowl-ing at them.

'Her father is here.'

It took a moment for the sheikh's words to penetrate her desire-fogged brain but when they did she gasped.

Here? As in, the palace *here?*

'What?' Zach's tone echoed her own disbelief.

'Yes. And he's after blood—yours, to be precise. I told you this would happen.'

Told him what would happen?

The prince released her and stepped back, a victorious, snake charmer's grin on his face. 'He'll get blood, but it won't be mine.'

A lightning streak of fear shot through Farah. 'What are you going to do to him?'

Ignoring her, Zach raised a hand and a nearby guard materialised at his side. 'Take Miss Hajjar to the harem.'

She grabbed his forearm. 'I want to see my father.'

'Don't let her out of your sight,' he continued as if she hadn't spoken. 'Not even for a second.'

Nadir stayed the guard before he could move. 'Unfortunately I told her father I would bring her.'

'Why would you do that?' the prince snapped at him.

Nadir's brow rose and Farah wasn't sure if it was with censure or surprise. 'He wants to see her for himself.'

'I don't care.'

'I do.' This time the look was definitely censure. 'This is my wedding night, Zach,' he said grimly. 'You need to take care of this quickly and smoothly before Imogen realises something is amiss.'

The new king's care of his bride made Farah's stomach clench. Men did not put their women first, in her experience.

'Fine,' the prince growled. 'Let's get this over with.'

Farah tensed at the ominous ring in those words. In Bakaan, the prince wouldn't need a court order to have her father imprisoned or put to death, and desolation overtook her as she realised that, despite all her efforts, there was next to nothing she could do to save him now.

CHAPTER EIGHT

FARAH'S HEART CAUGHT in her throat as she saw her father standing proud and tall in what looked like a private office. Amir was beside him, four palace guards surrounding them both.

Her father's eyes fell on her and widened before turning to the prince. 'What have you done to my daughter?'

Farah felt the prince's barely leashed anger. 'Greetings to you, too, Hajjar,' he drawled insolently. 'How good of you to grace us with your presence.'

Her father's eyes narrowed. 'Just answer the question, cur.'

Farah nearly groaned at her father's rudeness. Now was not the time to challenge the man he had kidnapped.

'You will not be making demands here, Hajjar,' the prince said with grim certainty. 'You are in my realm now.'

Her father raised his head. 'I'm sure you will do your worst, but not to my daughter.'

'I'll do what I like.'

'Gentlemen.' Sheikh Nadir stepped between them. 'I urge you to keep this civil.'

'This is not one of your boardrooms, Nadir,' the prince overrode his brother. 'I intend to see justice done.'

'Justice?' Her father spat. 'You wouldn't know justice if it jumped up and bit you in the backside. You're just like your father.'

'Careful, Hajjar.' Sheikh Nadir's tone was unmistakably deadly. 'This is my wedding day and you did kidnap my brother.'

'I don't deny it. But he took my daughter and spent two nights with her alone in the desert. That is a slur against her good reputation and he should be forced to make amends.'

Amir shifted forward. 'Did you touch her?' he bit out.

Farah's eyes flew to his. A muscle jumped in his jaw as he eyeballed the prince.

'That's none of your business.' Prince Zachim's piercing gaze cut from Amir's to hers and Farah felt her face turn brick red as she recalled every time he *had* touched her and how much she had secretly enjoyed it. A spark of awareness simmered behind the prince's eyes, as if he knew exactly what she was thinking, as if he too could still feel the press of his blunt fingertips against the underside of her breasts. An unexpected shaft of hunger tightened every one of her nerves, as if in anticipation of that touch, and she released the shaky breath she'd been holding for too long. She knew she should be saying something but she couldn't move under the weight of that unmistakably sexual look; couldn't *think*.

'By Allah!' Her father's righteous bellow filled the room and Farah shook off the sensual malaise that threatened to consume her. 'If this cur has compromised my daughter's honour then he will marry her.'

Marry her?

'No!' Farah's automatic response was nearly drowned out by Prince Zachim's insulting laugh and Amir's horrified shout of disapproval.

'If you think you can use this to get out of justice being served, Hajjar, you're wrong,' Zach stated menacingly.

'At least I admit what I did,' her father spat, as if that completely exonerated him from his crime. 'You…you take my daughter and dress her up as your…your *whore* and expect me to say nothing?'

Even though she knew her father hadn't meant to insult her quite so badly, Farah still felt the sting of his disapproval like a sharp slap. The prince stilled beside her. 'Retract that insult to your daughter immediately,' he warned quietly. 'Or I will do it for you.'

Farah stiffened with shock at his instant and unequivocal defence of her. It felt as if no one had been in her corner since her mother had died and a sweet spear of pain lanced her heart.

'Do you deny the charge?' her father demanded.

'I am not beholden to you or anyone else,' the prince stated grimly.

'But you are beholden to the laws of this country and you have wronged my daughter by taking her from her home and then spending the night with her. And something happened between you,' her father asserted. 'My daughter is in shock.'

An understatement, Farah thought, her mind reeling at all that had been said, including the ludicrous statement that the prince should marry her. Her father had to be mad to even suggest it.

'Zach?' Nadir's quietly controlled voice broke into the emotion swirling around them and something passed between the two brothers that she couldn't read.

Prince Zachim growled low in his throat and stabbed a hand through his jet-black hair, the lethal glitter in his amber gaze pinning her to the spot. Power throbbed from every one of his muscles and the sexual chemistry that thrilled her as much as it appalled her ratcheted up a notch. 'I did not compromise this woman,' he said with deliberate slowness.

'Easy enough to say,' her father snarled.

'Tell him, Farah,' the prince ordered roughly, her name husky on his lips.

Tell me you want me, Farah?

'Tell him that nothing happened between us.'

Nothing?

She blinked up at him. She supposed in his world the way he had touched her and kissed her had meant nothing to him and, no, he hadn't compromised her in the way her father meant. But he had made her aware of the sensual nature of her body for the first time in her life and it had changed her in a way she couldn't yet explain. Worse, it had made her want him on a level she had never wanted another man. Was that nothing?

Appalled to find herself close to tears, she stared at the floor to gather her wits but as soon as she heard Amir's swift intake of breath she realised that the men had interpreted her hesitation as an admission of guilt.

A clock she hadn't noticed before ticked loudly in the deathly silence right before both her father and Amir erupted, gesticulating wildly. Within seconds the palace guards surrounded them, guns drawn.

Farah saw Prince Zachim stiffen as he stared at her, his expression one of outraged astonishment. Sheikh Nadir swore under his breath.

'By Allah, you will marry my daughter,' her father bellowed, 'or you will bring the wrath of all the mountain tribes down on your head.'

The sheikh swore again.

So did the prince this time.

'Father, listen, I—'

'Stay out of this, Farah.'

Stay out of it! Farah nearly choked as her own temper rose to the surface.

Then Amir spoke, further tightening the screws of tension in the elegant room. 'I will marry Farah.'

Farah groaned. 'Amir, don't.'

His brown eyes were fierce as they met hers. 'I don't care if you have lain with him. I will have you for my own.'

'Over my dead body.' The prince hadn't moved a muscle but he seemed to dominate the space.

Farah's head throbbed as her mind scrambled to fix what was happening.

'Zach. A word.' Nadir's commanding tone brooked no argument. Farah glanced away as the prince gave her a loaded stare before following his brother to the other side of the room.

Sighing heavily, she rounded on her father. 'Father—'

'Don't argue.' He folded his arms across his massive chest. 'That dog will do the honourable thing by you if it's the last thing he does.'

'But I don't want to get married,' she asserted.

Her father waved her claim away as if her desires were inconsequential. 'Every woman wants to get married.'

Well aware of his chauvinistic views, Farah tried another tact. 'At least let me choose who I marry, because the prince was telling the truth—*nothing* happened.'

'You should have listened to me,' her father stated as if she hadn't even spoken. 'When I told you to stay away from him.'

'Like you're listening to me now?' she retorted.

'I told you to stay away, too.' Amir interrupted, clasping her clammy hands between his. 'I knew it would lead to trouble.'

So this was her fault?

She felt so utterly infuriated she didn't trust herself to speak. And she supposed this *was* her fault, in a way. She *had* defied her father in her misguided attempt to fix everything but, damn it, she had only wanted to help. She had only wanted to prevent things from getting worse for her father. Next time he wanted to go rampaging she'd make sure she stayed home!

She stared down at Amir's hands holding hers, his thumb stroking her skin in a soothing gesture, and she wondered how much more this night would deteriorate when the high and mighty Prince of Bakaan refused to marry her.

'Zach, you don't have to marry her.'

Zach heard Nadir's quiet words but his attention was riveted to the tableau across the room. Their body language spoke volumes. Farah's face flushed with her ardent displeasure; her bearing was nothing short of regal, her father holding himself aloof like an imperious ass, and his second-in-command…had just taken hold of her hands.

Zach's eyes narrowed. An unexplainable rage welled up inside him. Were they secret lovers? It wasn't unheard of, even though a woman was supposed to come to her husband's marriage bed a virgin. Would she come to his in that untouched state? Or had she already given herself to the idiot who was about to lose his hand—at best!

His jaw clenched. 'Idiot.'

'Sorry?'

'Not you.' Zach briefly thought about bypassing his hand and going straight for his neck. He, the master communicator—well, there was nothing like a broken neck to get a point across, he supposed. 'But, yes, I do have to marry her.'

Nadir's expression grew stern. 'Bloody hell. I believed you when you said you hadn't slept with her. I should have known when I saw you in the garden—'

'That was nothing.'

'Nothing? Two more minutes and you would have ripped her clothes off.'

Zach drew his eyes away from Farah and regarded his brother. 'More like one, but that's not why I have to marry her. And I didn't lie. Nothing has actually happened between us.' Well, nothing if you ignored the unexpected make-out session in the alleyway or his subsequent fantasies in the shower. Not to mention what he'd been about to do to her in the garden. 'I have not slept with her. Not in the biblical sense, anyway.'

'Then we'll get you out of this.'

Zach could see Nadir readying himself to go into problem-solving mode but Zach's attention was elsewhere. Which was why he only vaguely heard the mention of war, peace and love. And he knew his brother wasn't doing a book review.

He swung back to Nadir. 'What about love?'

Nadir sighed impatiently. 'You said that was the only reason you would marry—if you were in love.'

Yeah, that was what he'd said once. But honour and integrity were just as important and he wasn't about to let this little spitfire who knew obscure facts about Roman history, and who intrigued him and made him laugh as no other woman ever had, take that from him. 'Excuse me,' he said to his brother, crossing the room before he'd even registered his intention.

His icy gaze went to the idiot's, his hand to Farah's elbow. 'This meeting is over,' he informed the tense trio.

Of course, she tried to pull away from him. 'I told my father—'

'I will marry your daughter.' He spoke over the top of her, clasping her elbow more firmly.

'Never thought I'd see the day a Darkhan would do the right thing,' the old man preached.

'Only because you probably don't recognise the gesture.'

Farah's knight-errant cleared his throat. 'I don't—'

Zach turned on Amir as he squared off against him and was clearly about to spill his guts. 'You are about to lose your head if you're not careful,' he bit out. 'Guards, put them in prison,' he ordered softly.

At the mention of prison his newly acquired fiancée came to life once more. 'No!'

She pulled out of his hold and rushed to stand in front of the two men like Joan of Arc facing off against the English at Orleans. 'You can't send them to prison.'

Any other time her loyalty might have impressed him. Just not this time. 'And just how do you propose to stop me?'

'Zach…' He heard his brother's cautioning tone but ignored it.

'Not even you could lock up your own father-in-law,' she announced belligerently.

Her father stiffened. 'That's enough, Farah!' he scolded. 'I don't need you to fight my battles for me.'

Zach stared at the woman in front of him, all willowy and beautiful, a touch of vulnerability in her eyes most would probably have missed. He'd noticed it earlier as well, when her father had insulted her, and it had made him want to protect her then, as it did now.

Unable to stop himself, he reached out and ran the back of his knuckles down the smooth line of her cheek. Her breath hitched and he didn't miss that, either. 'So tough, my little spitfire,' he murmured. 'So passionate.'

She knocked his hand away. 'About things I care about, yes.' Her voice was husky and made his body ache to have her.

'Hell.' His brother's low curse spoke volumes. 'She has a point, Zach, and I need to get back to Imogen. I'll let you go, Hajjar,' his brother informed the older man. 'But you put one foot out of line and I'll haul you into prison so fast your head will spin.'

A lead silence filled the room.

'Come, Farah,' her father finally said with a regal dignity that made Zach want to laugh. 'I will take you home.'

'No, you won't,' Zach found himself saying. He smiled. 'Your daughter is now my fiancée and that means she's mine to do with as I please.'

CHAPTER NINE

WITH THE RUSH of adrenaline behind him, Zach was seriously starting to question his sanity. He'd just committed himself to marry a woman he barely knew. A woman he didn't even like!

He stormed down the corridor with said woman in tow. How had this happened? One minute he'd been celebrating not only his brother's wedding but also the fact that Nadir had agreed to take the throne and the next he was...he was...getting married? Any minute now and he was sure doctors in white coats were going to come rushing around the corner looking for him.

The cause of his immense irritation tugged against his hold. 'I'm tired of you dragging me around like this.'

Zach tightened his grip. 'Not as tired as I am of having to do it.'

Especially when they were in this predicament because she hadn't spoken up and admitted that nothing had happened between them.

Nothing? his conscience mocked.

A growl rose up in his throat. A few kisses did not require a marriage proposal. In the West they might not, but in Bakaan a man didn't trifle with a woman unless he was serious.

But marry Farah Hajjar?

Zach inwardly cursed himself. All his life he'd ignored

the exotic Bakaani girls who had thrown themselves in his path with one purpose in mind. All his life, until this one. And she hadn't even thrown herself at him. No. She'd done something much worse: she'd kidnapped him. Or her father had.

He still didn't know why the old man had done it, although he could guess. With Zach's father gone, Hajjar had probably hoped to destabilise the country and attempt a coup. The thought was as ludicrous as his suggestion that Zach marry his daughter. And then another possibility hit him and his whole body went still.

Farah squeaked as she nearly ran into him from behind. Zach stared at her. Was that why Hajjar had done it? To get the two of them together so that they were forced to marry and get a Hajjar on the throne any way possible? His rational side discounted the idea as absurd—the Hajjars had hated the Darkhans since the dawn of time—but he'd underestimated Farah once before and had the scar on his arm to show for it. Had he underestimated her father, as well?

'We need to talk.' He pushed open the door to his apartment.

Farah glanced up at him as she swept past. 'I couldn't agree more.'

Dismissing his guards with a nod, Zach followed her inside. He bypassed his sofas, headed straight for his wet bar and grabbed a crystal decanter half filled with whisky. 'Drink?'

She eyed the offer disparagingly. 'I thought you wanted to talk.'

He downed a finger of Scotch. 'I'd like to dull the pain first.'

'We're not really getting married, you know.'

'We're not?' He added ice to the glass this time before leaning back against the bar, taking in her rigid stance.

'That whole thing was just an act back there? Damn, I wish I'd known. I would have organised party music.'

Her soft lips pinched together. 'Don't you know that sarcasm is the lowest form of wit?'

'It's fitting, then,' he drawled. 'Since I can't remember feeling this low before.'

'You and me both,' she said on a rush, sinking down onto one of the sofas and removing her heels; her sigh of pleasure hitting him exactly where he didn't need it to right now.

'You know, if you drop the kidnapping charges I could probably get my father to withdraw his demands that we marry.' Her pleading look was one of innocence and hope and for a fleeting moment he had to fight the urge to go and comfort her.

Clearing his head with another dose of alcohol, he cast her a cynical smile. 'Oh, I'm sure you'd like that,' he bit out. 'But it's not that simple any more.'

'I don't see why not.'

'Because your lack of a convincing denial that I have *dishonoured* you has set something bigger than the two of us in motion. But then, maybe you knew that all along,' he added softly.

'Knew what?'

Zach paced to shake off the adrenaline that surged through him. Her puzzled expression was either genuine or a good act. His money was on the latter. 'Marrying me has enormous benefits.'

'Like what?' She gave a derisive snort. 'Being close to your *enormous* ego?'

Unable to remember another woman who had dared to speak to him with such disdain, he stopped in front of her, forcing her to have to look a long way up to meet his gaze. 'Money. Power.' He gritted his teeth. 'A Hajjar potentially on the throne one day.'

Instead of being intimidated by him, she just looked annoyed. 'If you're implying that my father *wanted* this to happen…' She wrinkled her nose. 'That's ludicrous. He loathes your family.'

'He loathes that my family is on the throne, and now we're to be married. A bit opportune, don't you think?'

'No, I don't think that at all, and if you thought about it logically you'd know it's not true. My father is stuck in the past and thinks that all women need a man to take care of them. That's the only thing that's going on here.'

It wasn't the only thing going on here but perhaps he should have stopped at one whisky because what she said made sense. Not that he wouldn't put it past Hajjar to capitalise on a situation that had arisen as a result of his own poor judgment in lifting her onto that horse in the first place.

Zach crushed an ice block between his teeth. 'Unfortunately I don't feel particularly logical right now. And your father gets to go free with you as the sacrificial lamb.'

Her face paled. 'No, there has to be another way.'

'Why, so you can go off and marry your boyfriend, the knight, instead?' he asked silkily.

She frowned. 'Amir?' she finally said. 'No, I don't want to marry Amir or anyone, and given your reputation I'd think you would feel the same way.'

Zach stilled. 'My reputation?'

'We get magazines in the mountains,' she said loftily. 'And I think the amount of different women you've been photographed with speaks for itself.'

He gave a rough bark of laughter. 'You're making me out to be the bad guy here?'

'Are you saying you want to get married?'

'As a matter of fact, I was nearly married once.' Or at least he'd contemplated asking Amy to marry him, which was close enough for the purposes of putting this little heathen in her place. 'So, yes, I do want to get married—just not to you, Miss Hajjar.'

Her face went even paler before flooding with colour and he felt like an ass.

'I suppose it doesn't matter to you because you can have a hundred wives if you choose.'

'I admit that I have great stamina in the bedroom,' he drawled. 'But even I would struggle with a hundred women. But, regardless, that law is about to be repealed.'

Farah's eyes climbed her forehead. 'It is?'

'Yes. It's time Bakaan entered the twenty-first century and my brother and I intend to see that happen. By the look on your face, you don't agree.'

'No. I mean, yes, of course I agree.' She hesitated. 'I just didn't expect...'

'That I would think that way?' he finished when her words tapered off. 'Possibly it's not just your father who is stuck in the past.' And why her poor opinion of him rankled was beyond him.

'I am not stuck in the past.' She thrust her hands on her hips righteously.

Zach eyed her appreciatively as she stood before him in a full snit. 'Hit a chord did I?'

Yes, he had hit a chord, because she was a forward-thinking person, not a backward-thinking one. But she was so confused right now. His declaration that he'd been nearly married once before, and his adamant statement that he would never want to marry her, had somehow rocked her and she had no idea why. 'No, you have not hit a chord,' she denied hotly, staring into his too-cocky, too-handsome face. 'But I want to hit you and I'm a non-violent person!'

'So says the woman who attacked me with a sword.'

'Okay, fine—generally I'm a non-violent person. And

I'm sure if you could just reach into your heart and forgive my father and let this go—'

'Let bygones be bygones, you mean?'

'Yes, exact—'

'No.'

'Would you stop cutting me off?' She angled her chin at him. 'Can't you see that showing forgiveness puts you in the powerful position? If my father continues to act out against you unprovoked, then everyone is likely to turn on *him*.'

'Remind me which fairy story you derived that bit of whimsy from.'

Having him mock her made Farah grit her teeth together. 'Just because you don't believe in non-violent methods of communication doesn't mean you have to belittle ideas that have worked before. Ever heard of Martin Luther King? Ghandi? *Mother Teresa?*' She lobbed the names of some of her heroes at him. 'Perhaps if you open your mind up a bit more you might learn something.'

The look he gave her was ferocious. 'You have some nerve coming to me about non-violent methods of communication. Someone in your village started a publication five years ago that nearly incited a civil war. If I hadn't come home and settled things—in a *non-violent* manner, I might add—who knows how many people would have died?'

'I didn't mean to incite anything,' she countered.

'I didn't say you did, I said—' He stopped and stared at her. 'You started that provincial publication?'

Farah was instantly flooded with heat at his condescension. 'My magazine was not provincial, thank you very much!' She bit her tongue to stop herself from calling him every name she could think of, digging her toes into the soft pile rug beneath her feet.

'That's not possible,' he said, the incredulity in his voice beyond insulting. 'You would have only been a child when that was done.'

Farah's hands shot to her hips. 'I was seventeen!'

He shook his head, a frown on his face. 'There were a lot of sharp observations in that paper.'

'If you're expecting me to thank you for saying so, you'll be waiting a long time.' Like, forever. 'And I hardly think it's important.'

'Not important,' he growled, seemingly as angry as she was. 'It's the reason I had to return to Bakaan!'

'Something you obviously didn't want to do, by your tone.'

'Not when I had to give up control of my company and end my racing career, no.'

'I'm so sorry,' she simpered. 'How thoughtless of us—your people—to need you.'

'Yes, it was.' His voice lowered an octave and the skin on the back of her neck prickled with awareness. 'Although, I'm not completely unhappy that *you* need me.'

Attempting to ignore the suddenly charged atmosphere he was deliberately creating, she lifted her chin. 'I need you to install medical centres in our villages and provide educational materials so we don't have to sneak them from across the border or—' She stopped, suddenly aware that yet again he'd got her so incensed she was about to divulge sensitive information to him.

'Or what?' he asked softly. 'Get them from a secret source inside the palace?'

He knew about that! Farah tried to act nonchalant because she had no doubt that whoever had sent those items to them over the past couple of years would be punished. 'I don't know what you're talking about. But what I want to know is how we get out of this marriage.'

'We're not.'

The conviction in his tone chafed her already raw nerves. 'But we have to.'

'I don't know why you're fighting this so much. Your life is about to improve out of sight.'

'Improve?' She laughed, because what else could she do? 'That's because you're nothing but an arrogant, egotistical, high and mighty prince whose shoe size is larger than his IQ.'

His slow smile told her that her insults had landed on fallow ground. 'Careful, *habiba*, or I might start to think that you like me.'

Oh, but he had a way of pushing her buttons. 'That will never happen,' she assured him loftily.

'No?'

'No.'

'But you like my touch.' He came towards her all long, lean and muscular. 'Don't you, Farah?'

She swallowed hard. 'No.'

He paused and cocked his head. 'Have you forgotten what I said would happen the next time you denied you wanted me?'

'You know you're redefining the term "egotistical," don't you?'

He laughed. 'And you're redefining denial. But I find myself wondering why I'm denying myself something I've already been accused of taking.'

Farah's hands came up to ward him off, a thrilling sort of fear coursing through her as he kept coming until she was forced up against a wall, his towering body just inches from hers. He planted his hands by both sides of her head, caging her in. 'Give me one good reason, *habiba*, *one* good reason why I shouldn't unwrap you from that pretty dress and give you exactly what we both want?'

Feeling as if she'd just run a marathon, Farah could barely breathe let alone speak. All she wanted to do was smooth her hands up over his wide chest and finish what he had started back in the garden. The urge was almost overwhelming but she knew there would be no going back after that and she definitely wasn't ready for that.

'Tell me,' he said softly, 'How far did you and the knight go?'

Not sure what he was asking, she frowned, and then she caught the suggestive glint in his eyes and she knew. Struggling to get her thoughts in order with him this close, she frowned again. 'We haven't… I've never…'

A slow smile spread across his face. 'He didn't touch you.' He shook his head as if in wonder.

Knowing there was in insult buried in that look, she pushed at his chest, relieved when he let her pass. 'I won't do it,' she muttered, 'I refuse to marry you.'

'You have to.' His gaze turned implacable. 'Have you forgotten that my honour and your reputation are at stake?'

'No, but I don't care about my reputation!' she cried. Her vision of a future in which she directed her own life was falling away from her before her very eyes. If she couldn't do anything about it, she was going to be married, and she couldn't think of anything worse. Well, her father dying in a prison cell was worse, and perhaps never experiencing the prince's hot kisses again… But, no, how could that be worse?

'Well, I care about my honour,' he said coldly. 'Especially at a time when I need the support of our people. And let's not forget your father's small threat of war.'

'But—'

'Enough. I find I am exhausted from all the *excitement* of the past week, not to mention tonight. We will be married, Farah. Perhaps it is fate.'

A sense of inevitability stole over her at his words. She had always known there would be a price to pay for her father's actions; she just hadn't expected that price to be her marriage.

Shaking her head, she swallowed past a lump in her throat that extended all the way to her stomach. 'I've never liked fate,' she said dully.

The prince gave her a faintly mocking smile. 'While I have never believed in it. But it won't be all bad.' His tone softened. 'I will be gentle with you, *habiba*.'

Heat bloomed across her cheeks as she realised how exactly he was going to be gentle with her. 'I don't want you to be gentle with me,' she blazed. 'I don't want you to be anything with me.'

He smiled as if he knew better than she did. 'We'll see.'

CHAPTER TEN

THREE DAYS LATER Zach found himself a married man. Something he should have felt worse about, given that he wasn't in love with his bride, but didn't.

The wedding had been small, nothing like his brother's extravaganza, but everyone had said it was romantic, the way the prince had fallen in love with the daughter of his father's archenemy thus uniting what had once been the two biggest tribes in the country. Zach hadn't thought of it that way at the time it was going down, but the advantages were obvious on a political level. On a personal level his mother seemed to take great delight in the 'love match' so he had remained silent about the real reason behind their union.

A union he'd had the power to prevent when Nadir had informed him that he'd come up with a plan to extricate him from it. Zach knew it would have been what Farah wanted. Hell, it was what *he* wanted. So why hadn't he done it? Especially with his brother about to become the next king; it would have meant total freedom for him, which he had now firmly denied himself.

Nothing made sense, not the churning feeling in his gut, nor the way Farah made him feel so hungry for her. As if she was the last woman in the world for him.

Well, she is, his conscience reminded him, *and you will be the first man to touch her.*

Something he found himself increasingly impatient to do. Probably he should be a little worried about his eagerness to bed a woman who so obviously didn't like him, but he wasn't. They might not have started this marriage in a conventional way but he had no doubt that she would please him. As he would please her once she stopped being so prickly about everything.

She was an intriguing personality, his new wife—headstrong and handy with a sword, as well as brave and fiercely loyal, with a keen intelligence all tied up in one delectably feminine package he was straining to unwrap.

Nadir's comment about his deliberately choosing the wrong women in the past came back to him. Was it possible? He never would have said so before but he also knew that Amy had never stirred the level of feeling in him that Farah did.

Scanning the milling crowd he easily located Farah across the room talking with his mother. She looked striking in a long-sleeved cream gown that skimmed her slender frame and ended at the floor. A whiff of something far more insidious than desire curled through him as he watched her. It gave him pause and, as if sensing the swirl of emotion coursing through him, his lovely bride glanced at him from beneath her long lashes.

Her eyes flared briefly as he took her in and Zach could almost feel the shudder that went through her. As much as she might not like to admit it, she wanted him just as much as he wanted her. His blood heated, driving everything else out of his head except bedding her.

'Drink, little brother?'

Cursing under his breath, Zach arched a brow at his brother. He knew Nadir felt sorry for him. He knew he wasn't in love with Farah and since finding love himself he'd turned into some sort of agony uncle. But he didn't want a drink. He didn't want anything to dull his senses for his wedding night to come. 'No, I'm good.'

Was it too early to leave? He glanced at his watch. They'd been at the reception for an hour; surely that was long enough.

'Imogen was wondering where you intend to go for your honeymoon.'

Honeymoon? Interesting question and one he hadn't even considered. He'd spent the last three days in back to back meetings trying not to think about sex before marriage. Now he realised that a honeymoon would be the perfect excuse to take Farah away from the worries of Bakaan and the reason behind their marriage. A chance to start fresh.

But where to go? Paris? New York? The Seychelles? No, wrong time of year for— Suddenly Damian's birthday invitation swung into his mind. *Ibiza?* Could he take her to Ibiza?

'I wouldn't recommend it.'

Not realising he'd spoken out loud until Nadir replied, Zach frowned. 'Why not?'

'It's a bit…wild. But why would you— Ah…' His brother smiled. 'Offshore racing.'

Zach shrugged. 'I am still the team owner,' he pointed out. 'But it's Damian's birthday. I should be there.'

Nadir's brows rose. 'You're going to spend your honeymoon at a mate's birthday party?'

'Of course not,' Zach grated; he wasn't that selfish. 'The party is one night and we'll have the whole week. What's wrong with that?'

Nadir held up his hands at Zach's aggrieved expression. 'You're the expert on women, not me.'

'Glad you finally admit it,' Zach growled. Ibiza was the perfect idea: fun, carefree and totally different from Bakaan. What could possibly go wrong?

* * *

'The wedding was beautiful and you look especially lovely in your wonderful dress.'

'Thank you.' Farah automatically murmured the rote response she had given most of the well-wishers at the wedding even though the gentle woman who had just joined her was now her mother-in-law. The fact was her brain was operating in some sort of a fog. She kept reminding herself that she was doing this for her father but that didn't always feel like the truth and that worried her just as much as being married did.

'I hope you don't mind about the orchid.'

'The orchid?'

'A wedding gift from my private nursery. I had it delivered to your apartment in the palace. It's very rare but also very hardy. It represents love and fertility.'

Farah forced a smile at her words. Earlier Zach had asked her not to reveal the reason behind their marriage to his mother. She didn't know why, other than to stroke his massive ego, but she had agreed to go along with it. Now she felt like a phony as his mother beamed up at her. 'My son always said he would marry for love, and I am so glad he has, because he deserves it.'

Love? Farah never would have imagined that her new husband would be motivated by such a deep emotion and it made her wonder if he had been in love with the woman he had almost married. And if he had been in love then, was he still? She clutched her stomach, feeling a little ill at the thought. Or was that just the bubbly drink she'd consumed? Imogen had warned her to go easy on it but it was so sweet and refreshing she kept forgetting. She took another sip and realised that her mother-in-law was waiting for her to say something.

Wondering if 'thank you' was even mildly appropriate, she was almost glad when Zach approached them.

'I hope my mother is not making your ears bleed, *habiba*?' He smiled down at her like any indulgent new husband who was indeed in love with his wife.

'Not at all,' she said a little breathlessly, trying to remember how much she disliked his handsome face.

She noticed the loving look he bestowed on his mother and suddenly wondered if his wish to keep his mother in the dark about their union had less to do with his ego and more to do with real caring. She'd lived on a diet of her father's prejudices against this man and his family for so long it was difficult to differentiate fact from fiction where he was concerned. His comment that perhaps her father wasn't the only one living in the past returned but she shook it off. She absolutely did not live in the past.

Grumpily, she watched his mother return his smile as if the sun shone out of him and Farah felt a pang that her own mother wasn't present. Probably if she had been, then Farah wouldn't have been here because her father would not have been bitter enough to kidnap the prince.

She glanced across the room to where her father was talking with a group of men, seeming to have forgotten the events that had led them to this night. He was the only person from her village present because Farah hadn't wanted to invite anyone else. It wasn't as if this was a real celebration and now she wished she had at least invited her good friend, Lila. She could do with the moral support, if not some advice about her wedding night to come.

The thought of sleeping with the prince caused a riot of mixed emotions to take flight in her stomach and she sipped her drink to subdue them. Should she be looking forward quite so much to joining with a man she didn't like? And would it be as good as kissing him was, or would it be a let down, as she'd heard other women tell of it? Somehow she knew that it wouldn't be and she shivered.

'Cold, *habiba*?' Zach leant closer to her and she shook her head. She wasn't cold, she was hot. Too hot.

As if he was completely attuned to her innermost thoughts, his hand splayed possessively across her hip. 'I'm afraid we have to leave you, Mother. We have a honeymoon to get to.'

'Oh, how romantic. Make me lots of babies.'

Honeymoon? Babies? Farah's stomach fluttered again. All this talk of love and seeing Imogen and Sheikh Nadir's obvious adoration for each other was making her think strange, unwanted thoughts about things she'd once steadfastly declared she did not want, things that would make her just as beholden to a man as any other Bakaani woman. Things that had her earlier panic about marriage return tenfold.

Before she could tell him she had no desire to go on a honeymoon like a real married couple, his nose grazed the top of her head. 'You smell delicious,' he murmured huskily. 'What scent did you bathe in?'

Farah didn't want to remember her bath. Four women had come to prepare her for his pleasure and it had been like negotiations in a war room as they'd massaged and plucked and waxed her body into submission. Farah had determinedly refused to allow them to touch the hair between her legs and they'd clucked and tsked like old hens trying to establish the pecking order. The prince would not approve, they'd said. Good, she'd replied, much to their consternation. Now she wondered if he would approve and she hated the feeling of weakness that underscored that thought, hated the desire that she wanted to please him at all. She didn't. She didn't care what he thought of her.

She lifted her chin. 'Poison.'

'Then I will die a happy man tonight.'

His husky chuckle made her nerves tighten and Farah raised her half-empty glass to her lips. 'One can only hope.'

But he wasn't listening, instead he was frowning at her glass. 'Perhaps you should think about switching to water.'

'But I like this very much.' She tilted the glass to her lips in what she knew was a childishly defiant gesture and drained it. 'What is it called again?' She felt slightly dizzy from the rush of alcohol as it hit her stomach, but it was worth it to see him scowl.

'Champagne.' His frown deepened. 'Have you even had it before?'

'Loads of times. We distil it in the hut behind my father's.'

His eyes narrowed and Farah widened hers innocently. Then he completely surprised her by shaking his head and laughing softly. 'Okay, I deserved that.'

And there he went again, throwing her off just when she thought she had him all worked out.

'Come, Farah, we should go.'

Oh, yes, the honeymoon.

Suddenly nerves attacked her. She'd been deliberately not thinking about the end of the evening and what would come next. 'I think it would be rude to leave so soon,' she said, aiming for cool and knowing she'd missed by a mile when his lips twisted in sympathy. *Sympathy!*

'Actually, it's quite late.'

Heat raced through her, making her feel even dizzier than she already was.

'Where are we going?'

'So suspicious, wife.' He smiled. 'We are going to Ibiza.'

'Ib… Where?'

'It's a small, ruggedly beautiful island off the coast of Spain. You'll love it.'

She raised an eyebrow. She had always wanted to travel to faraway places but had never imagined she'd ever get the chance. 'Because you say I will?'

She hadn't realised she'd raised her chin until he gripped it and tugged it down, his thumb resting on the curve of her lower lip. Her nerves were so raw even that small contact made her insides fizz.

'I know you want another argument but I'm not going to give you one,' he said. 'It's time to make love, Farah, not war. Wouldn't you prefer that?' His voice was a rough caress against her ear and before she could tell him that, actually, she was quite happy with war, he placed his hand firmly against the small of her back. Her breath caught and a delicious tingle of anticipation followed his fingers as they slid upwards to grip the nape of her neck. It was a blatantly possessive hold and spoke of domination and ownership. Farah, who had never imagined wanting to experience either of those things, felt every one of her bones turn to water.

Half an hour later they were ensconced on the royal plane and she was trying not to ogle the sleek luxury of the streamlined jet. 'Where are all the seats?' she asked, taking in the well-spaced leather chairs and small tables.

'This is a private plane. You'll need to take a seat when we take off. After that you can walk around the cabin. There's a bedroom in the back and two bathrooms. Are you okay?'

'I'm not sure.' Her hand went to her head. 'I think I have a headache.'

'Already?' His smile was faintly mocking. 'I've heard it takes wives a little longer to start producing that ex—'

'Oh...' Farah moaned and must have turned as green as she felt because Zach forced her head down between her knees. 'Oh, that's worse.'

'It's the champagne.'

She waited for the nausea to pass and then sat up slowly. 'How can something that tastes so lovely make me feel so ill?'

'You're meant to drink it in small doses.'

'Small doses, like small steps,' she hiccupped.

'Exactly.' She heard the smile in his voice but kept her eyes closed.

'I think I'm okay now.'

'Just lie back.'

The plane chose that moment to accelerate down the runway and Farah's stomach revolted as they were lifted into the air. 'Oh, no I— Oh!'

Before she registered what was happening, she was in Zach's arms and then she was bent over a toilet bowl and emptying the contents of her stomach—which was thankfully very little, since she'd been too nervous to eat during the reception.

'I think I hate champagne,' she mumbled, so wretched she couldn't even muster any embarrassment.

His soft laugh was vaguely reassuring. 'I thought you loved it.'

'Not any more.'

'Unfortunately, you're likely to feel even worse tomorrow.'

'Please feel free to shoot me if I do.'

'I don't want to shoot you, *habiba*,' he said so softly she almost didn't catch it.

She took the glass of water he offered and drank deeply. When she was finished, she was only vaguely aware of him lifting her and carrying her to a cool, flat surface. She buried her head against something warm and firm. A pillow?

She felt her hair being released from the confines of her twist and moaned softly when he threaded his fingers through it.

'I love your hair.'

She frowned but didn't open her eyes. 'You do?'

'Yes. And your eyebrows.' He swept a finger over each one. 'Like the wings of a raven in full flight. And your nose—'

'My nose is too prominent.'

He ran his finger down the fine blade. 'It suits your face. And your mouth…'

Farah yawned and snuggled further into the pillow that smelled just like the prince. For some reason she felt completely relaxed and safe, as if she didn't have anything in the world to worry about. It was such a novel experience she let it wash over her. 'What about my mouth?' she asked, her mind drifting toward sleep.

'Your mouth.' He paused. 'Let's just say your mouth keeps me up nights.'

'Mmm, that's nice.'

He chuckled. 'I'm glad you think so.'

He stoked her hair and Farah floated into another realm, trying to cling on to whatever it was the prince was saying, but quite unable to do so.

When she finally regained consciousness she was instantly flooded with alarm. She should be helping to get water down by the well; she should be fixing breakfast. Then the softness of the bed she was in permeated her hazy state and she opened her eyes and saw floaty white curtains across the room being ruffled by a gentle breeze. Used to gaging her surroundings by scent, she breathed in deeply. The air was humid rather than dry and held a tinge of brine to it. A balminess.

Her mind started recollecting all the moments that had led to this one but there was a gaping hole between her throwing up on Zach's luxuriously appointed plane to lying in a bed that was as big as her whole room growing up.

And where was he? Because she could already tell that he had not slept beside her last night. Rising up on her elbows, she gingerly shifted her head from side to side to test the headache. Fortunately it didn't hurt but her mouth felt like she'd stuffed cotton into it and she was thirsty. Which was probably why she'd woken up thinking about water.

Pushing the linen sheet aside, she frowned when she realised she was only wearing her underwear. Did that mean Zach had undressed her last night or did he have an army of servants in this place, as well?

Flicking the bathroom light on against the gray haze of early morning, she was surprised to see that she looked pretty normal, except for the smudge of kohl around her eyes and her mussed hair. Wiping away the make-up, and brushing her teeth with the new toothbrush that stood in a small gold jar on the marble sink, she set about trying to tidy her hair. Deciding it was impossible, she was about to leave the room when she caught sight of herself in a full-length mirror. The underwear she'd been given for the wedding was pure white and as delicate as a finely spun spider's web. The bra was demi-cup, the panties cut high on her hips and completely sheer, somehow making the dark curls they hid look tempting and erotic. Shaking off the unnerving spark of arousal that thought caused, she truly hoped a servant had undressed her and not Zach.

Really? A little voice taunted.

No... She grimaced at the battle inside her head, grabbed a white robe she spied hanging from the back of the door and belted it tightly around her waist. She didn't hope that. Much to her chagrin, part of her hoped that Zach had undressed her and that he'd liked what he'd seen.

But where was he?

Asleep on the deep divan in the adjoining room, as it turned out. His large frame was sprawled on his back, his bare feet hanging over the edge. At some point he must have changed because he was no longer wearing his wedding robes but low-riding sweatpants and nothing else... And, oh, but he was built.

Farah stilled, taking him in. She wanted to go to him and run her hands all over his gloriously golden-brown skin, petting the dark pelt of hair on his chest right where it arrowed down the centre of his lean torso like a tempting trail. Of course, she didn't. She couldn't think straight enough to unglue herself from the doorway for a start.

'You're awake.'

Farah's eyes flew to his. So was he.

Obviously.

She swallowed, feeling vulnerable at having been caught staring at him. 'Yes.'

He stifled a yawn. 'It's early.' His eyes held hers, gleaming in the faint light.

'I'm sorry did I...did I wake you?'

'Not really. This sofa isn't the most comfortable to sleep on.'

'Oh, you should have...' She gestured vaguely to the bedroom behind her. He was her husband. He would be sleeping with her from now on. Yesterday the thought had been horrifying but right now she couldn't muster that same sense of dread.

'Did you undress me?' Her face flamed as soon as the words left her mouth. What was wrong with her? 'I mean—'

'Yes, I undressed you.'

'Oh.' She gripped the lapels of her robe together and glanced around, only vaguely aware of the beautifully appointed room cast in morning shadows. 'I thought maybe you had servants.'

'No.' He swung his feet to the floor and stood up. Farah's eyes returned to his large frame and her heart took off. 'No servants here.'

Had he been that tall yesterday? That imposing? She suddenly felt very thirsty again. 'Oh, well.' She waved a hand around aimlessly. 'I didn't mean to wake you.' *Especially not when you're only half-clothed.*

'I already said that you didn't wake me.'

Right. So he had.

'How's the head?'

It took her a minute to realise he was referring to her drunken episode on the plane. 'Um, good.' His gaze dropped to the belt on her robe and she realised she was fidgeting with it. 'So, thank you for taking care of me last night.'

A muscle knotted in his jaw. 'My pleasure.'

The softness of his tone thumped into her breastbone, his tone full of sensual promise and a decadent passion she was finding harder and harder to resist.

But for some reason it seemed imperative that she did resist, some deep awareness warning her that it was too much. That he made her feel too much. And as if to prove her own point her nipples peaked beneath her robe as if he were already touching her, the delicate fabric of her bra chafing like sandpaper, yet not rough enough to ease the ache. Would his hands be able to do that? His mouth? Involuntarily her eyes lifted to his.

A gruff sound broke the heavy silence between them and Farah realised that her husband was no longer standing stationary across the room. He was moving, towards her, his long, panther-like strides eating up the space between them.

Farah didn't move. She couldn't. She just waited, and if she'd thought her breathing shallow before, that was nothing compared to now. When he reached her he stopped and tucked a strand of her hair behind her ear.

The gesture tugged at her heartstrings. 'Do you…do you want coffee?' she asked on a nervous rush, her whole body taut with equal parts desire and dread.

'Coffee?' He shook his head. 'No, my beautiful bride, I do not want coffee.' He forked his fingers into the loose tumble of her hair. 'I want you.' He eased her forward until all that separated them was the thick cloth of her robe and his sweats. 'Naked.' She shuddered, completely mesmerised by the hunger burning in his eyes. 'Untie the robe.'

Like someone in a daze, Farah fumbled with the knotted belt until the lapels hung straight down. She saw his nostrils flare and a thrill raced down her spine.

'Now open it,' he urged roughly.

Slowly, feeling as if she was in a hot whirlpool about to go under, Farah did, and then she was hard up against him, the tips of her breasts crushed against the solid wall of his chest. She made a sound, more like a whimper, and her knees gave out.

'Yes,' he growled right before he dragged her mouth up to his and kissed her.

CHAPTER ELEVEN

IT MIGHT HAVE been because of the mystical aspect of the predawn morning or it might have been because of the state of her nerves—probably it was just him—but Farah gave up all thought of resisting. Instead she opened to him, lost in the mindless passion that he had started inside her.

Raising her arms she wound them around his neck and arched into his rough, restless hands as they skated over her back and met at her bottom, lifting her onto her toes.

He growled low, the sound rough and exciting. Her body answered it with a flood of moisture at her core. Fevered, Farah clutched at his shoulders, lifting herself higher, her body searching for that perfect alignment with his, that perfect amount of pressure that would ease the ache. Oh, there it was, right there! 'Zachim!'

He swallowed his name with his kiss and brought both hands up to cup her breasts. Farah nearly died as pleasure knifed through her. She arched more fully against him, seeking more, wanting—oh, yes, wanting—him to lightly pinch her nipples. Her body bowed toward his, seeking more. Had anything ever felt this good, this perfect? She nuzzled her nose against his neck, planting open-mouthed kisses along his jaw, his cheek, wherever she could reach.

He turned his head, his mouth capturing hers again, his hands squeezing her gently, his fingers teasing, one muscled thigh wedged between hers, stroking the flames higher.

Suddenly his touch on her breasts wasn't enough and she nearly whimpered with ecstasy as his hand trailed over her stomach and curved between her legs. She felt like she was standing on some kind of tightrope, her whole body like a finely tuned instrument waiting for the master player to stroke the correct parts, her focus completely centred on the heat of his palm cupping her.

He hitched her higher, one arm hooked below her bottom as he bent forward and took her nipple into his mouth, sucking hard. Farah cried out and clutched at him to hold him close.

'So beautiful. So...sweet.' He rolled her nipple between his teeth and then drew on her rhythmically, his fingers playing with the lace of her panties between her legs. Dimly she thought that she should stop him and then her brain reminded her that they were married. That he was allowed to touch her like this. That she was allowed to lift her hips towards his hand and widen her stance to make it easier for him to... She groaned long and low and her head hit the wall when his fingers slid beneath the lace.

Which was when she remembered, and her head snapped forward. 'I didn't— That is, I'm not—' She clamped one hand over his to stay his exploration.

'You're not what, *habiba*?'

His finger moved along the folds of her most private place and she completely forgot what she was or what she wasn't. Nothing mattered except the delicious sensations he evoked as he stroked her and pressed deep.

With her eyes blissfully closed, Farah was completely unprepared when Zach dropped to his knees and ripped her flimsy panties from her body.

Her eyes flew to his. 'Oh. I... You...'

'Shhh,' he whispered, lifting one of her thighs and draping it over his shoulder, opening her to him. 'I need to taste you.'

Lost in a rush of liquid heat Farah gripped his hair as his tongue lapped at her, part of her wanting to pull him away and another, much more wanton part, wanting to pull him in closer.

The wanton part won out and he rewarded her with long firm strokes of his tongue. 'That's it, *habiba*, let yourself go.' His lips latched on to a part of her that made her body tighten with anticipation and she no longer knew exactly what he was doing to her or what part of himself he was doing it with, every cell in her body assaulted by a kaleidoscope of sensation it was stretching to reach. 'You taste so good,' he crooned between licks. 'Hot and sweet.'

'Zachim, Zach—please, please, I…' She didn't know what she was asking him for but suddenly she screamed as sensation ripped through her body, holding her for one brief, paralysing moment before tossing her into a maelstrom of pleasure that had her falling, falling…

'I've got you.' Dimly she was aware of his hand between her legs, of his fingers pushed up inside her, locking her into place, absorbing the shudders that wouldn't seem to stop while he held her against him.

She could hear her own harsh breathing but she couldn't stop it. Couldn't… 'What did you just do to me?'

His mouth lingered on hers, easing her back down to earth. 'I gave you an orgasm.' Masculine satisfaction coated each word.

'Oh.' Farah licked her lips. She could taste him there and also herself.

'Good, yeah?'

She felt her already hot cheeks catch fire.

'It's okay, sweetheart. I want to do that again—have you come in my mouth. I want— Hell.' He swore and muttered something about a bed before scooping her up in his arms.

'What's wrong?'

'I just remembered that you haven't done this before.

I don't know how I forgot.' He twisted the doorknob and shouldered open the door. 'I'm sorry if I scared you.'

Farah buried her head against his shoulder and inhaled his male scent. He hadn't scared her, exactly. 'It was nice.'

'Nice? That was more than nice.' He placed her on the bed and slipped off her bra. Completely naked now, Farah stared up at him. A muscle flicked in his jaw.

'You're exquisite.' He came down over the top of her and lashed the tip of her naked breasts with his tongue. The sensation was so piercing Farah nearly shot off the bed. 'Oh. Oh. Do that again. Please...'

'With pleasure, *habiba*,' he purred against her aroused flesh. 'With pleasure.'

Her tiny little panting breaths were going to be the end of him, Zach decided as he tried to keep from yanking off his sweats and driving straight into her nude body. Especially with her squirming beneath him like she was.

He placed a hand on her hip to stay her, wanting to draw out the moment, wanting to memorise every dip and curve of her silky skin. Wanting to feast on her tight little nipples that were now the colour of dark berries from where he'd sucked them—and they were just as sweet. As was every part of her; he wanted to lick and kiss her all over, starting with her mouth and ending with his face buried deep between her thighs again. The way she had come apart before, the shock widening her chocolate-brown eyes as she'd reached the absolute pinnacle of pleasure for the first time, would stay with him always.

'Zachim?' Her voice was soft, questioning, and he realised he was staring at her.

He drew a lazy circle around the swells of her breasts. 'What do you want, sweetheart?' He lapped at her. 'More of this?'

'Yes, oh, yes!' she gasped. 'But I want… I want to see you. To touch you.'

He'd be damned if he didn't want that, too. 'I'm all yours.' He sat up and stilled when he felt her small hands lift to his chest. She smoothed them over him, testing the firmness of his muscles, the springiness of his chest hair. He worked out regularly, so he knew he was in shape, but watching her avid face as she took him in was a pleasure all by itself. Who would have known?

Her movements grew bolder as she worked her hands over his shoulders and down his arms, then back up to stroke them down his happy trail. Every muscle in his body tensed as she stopped at his sweats riding low on his hips. His erection was so hard he was surprised he hadn't burst a seam.

Unable to wait any longer, he came over the top of her. She looked up at him, her eyes questioning. 'I want to make this last,' he said thickly, bending his head and nipping at her lips. She opened instantly and Zach moaned, settling his weight on top of her.

She wound her arms around his neck and he widened her legs and gently slid a finger along her damp curls to test her readiness. She was still hot and slick and he had to bite back a low groan, pleased when a whimper escaped her lips and she raised her hips to meet his gentle thrusts. 'You like that?' He inhaled her aroused scent. 'You like it when I touch you?'

'Yes, oh, yes.' She widened her knees even more and Zach slipped another finger inside her tight sheath, preparing her for his possession. Sweat broke out over his forehead and his muscles shook with the effort to hold himself back.

He watched her eyes glaze over and felt masculine pride that he could get her so close to the edge again so quickly. She was his. All his. Her dark hair was a messy cloud around her head, her slender limbs quivering for more. So he gave it to her, bending his head to tongue her nipple while circling her clitoris with his thumb. She nearly came off the bed and he growled his appreciation and took the tight bud deeper. He went from one to the other until she was writhing and moaning on the bed.

'Zachim, I need more. Please. I want—'

'Me,' he finished for her. 'Only me.'

Rearing up, he quickly stripped the sweats from his legs and noticed her eyes widen at the sight of him. 'Don't worry, *habiba*, we will fit together.'

She swallowed. 'I don't know how.'

Zach smoothed her sweat-dampened hair from her face. 'I'll make it good for you. Open your legs for me, Farah,' he instructed after she had closed them at the sight of him.

Gently nudging her knees wide with his own he settled his hips between her thighs. She was so wet the tip of his erection slid a little way into her without him meaning to. She lifted against him and he stilled. 'Easy, *habiba*, I don't want to hurt you.'

He felt her muscles clamp down around him and his body shuddered as it fought for control. Barely holding back he leaned down to kiss her. When he felt her attention absorbed by his mouth, he slid in a little deeper, gritting his teeth as her soft heat surrounded him. By Allah, but going slow was torture. 'Sweetheart, *habiba*, just relax a little more for me.'

Sweat slicked his skin as she shifted beneath him and it was all he could do not to drive into her with one wild, brutal thrust home.

'Zachim...'

She lifted against him and it was Zach's undoing. 'I'm sorry, sweetheart, but I have to—' He slid deep and heard her gasp.

He stilled, waiting for her to push him away. Instead

she stroked his slick shoulders, his back, reaching down to cup his buttocks.

Zach pulled out a little way and pushed back in. She was hot, wet and so soft beneath him. So responsive. 'How are you? Does it hurt?'

'No, I... It feels like you're filling me up.'

'I am, sweetheart.' Zach withdrew and plunged into her a little more roughly. 'I'm all the way in.'

She gasped his name and something primal uncoiled inside him. Something unsettling, like a whispered warning. Tensing he tried to catch the essence of it but Farah lifted to him, trying to match his rhythm, and he stopped thinking and helped her, guiding her, learning her, his brain focused on only one objective.

He could feel the slight tremors of her contractions and sense the urgency of her impending orgasm as her body pushed up to meet his. The pleasure was so intense he lost all sense of control, his body driven by an ancient instinct that threw them both over the edge into a place he'd never known was possible.

For a long time afterwards, Zach lay staring at the ceiling, Farah asleep at his side, wondering if he'd ever experienced anything like what had just happened. Wondering if the world had ever stopped at the point of his joining with a woman before. Wondering if he had ever felt this sense of completion before, this happy.

It seemed like a ludicrous emotion to have in bed. Satisfaction, yes. Pleasure, a given. But completion? Joy? *Possessiveness?*

He turned onto his side and tucked a silky strand of her hair behind her ear. She sighed and curled closer. Zach rubbed his chest, too tired to think let alone analyse what he was feeling. What did it matter anyway? It was what it was. Farah was his wife and there was no going back now.

* * *

Blinking against a room filled with light, Farah slowly opened her eyes and listened to the distant street noises that told her she should have been up hours ago. Then she remembered why she wasn't in such glorious, technicolour detail that she wasn't sure if she should feel appalled or delighted. Certainly she'd never experienced that kind of pleasure in her life before.

She pulled a face as she recalled every one of her whimpers, moans and cries for more. Then there was the way she had stroked the downy line of hair that covered Zach's rocky abdomen... She'd been out of control. Internal muscles ached in agreement and she wondered how she was going to face him this morning. For a woman who claimed she hadn't wanted to get married or have a man in her life, she'd put up very little resistance.

Actually, a little voice pointed out helpfully, *you put up none.*

Great. Even better.

Showering and washing her hair quickly, she dried off and then realised she had nothing to wear. Hearing a noise in the next room, she cast around and saw her folded wedding dress on a chair against the wall. She'd feel silly putting that on. Then she noticed a T-shirt draped over the back of a chair.

It was red and had a white image of a bird of prey in full flight on the front. It smelt of Zach and she inhaled deeply, her internal muscles softening even more. She frowned. Should she be thinking of sex again so soon? Was this even normal?

Determined that she would not turn into one of those clingy women who lived only to serve her husband, Farah pushed her thick hair back over her shoulder and opened the bedroom door, hoping at least that Zach had more clothes on than earlier.

Unfortunately not; she inwardly groaned. He was standing, half-turned away from her, slicing something at the kitchen bench and wearing low-riding denims, his hair slightly damp as if he, too, was not long out of the shower; his torso and feet were bare.

The leap in her pulse was instant and she drew in a deep breath, the scent of bacon and coffee making her stomach rumble. Hearing the embarrassingly loud noise, Zach turned towards her, his leonine eyes raking her from head to toe in that intense way that made her body burn.

He cursed, a swift, harsh sound, before he brought the side of his thumb up to his mouth.

Realising what had happened, she rushed to his side. 'Oh no, did you just cut yourself?'

She took his hand in hers, examining the line of blood that appeared as soon as he stopped sucking on it. 'You need to wash this under running water so we can see how deep it is.'

'It's not deep.'

But he complied and Farah tested the skin around the cut. He was right. It wasn't deep. 'It will still need a plaster. Do you have one?'

'No idea.' His eyes darkened as he watched her. 'Don't you think it's strange that I always seem to bleed around you?'

'That only happened once before,' she said indignantly. 'And you can hardly hold me responsible for this incident.'

'You walk in wearing nothing but my T-shirt, what do you expect? It's more of a weapon than the damned sword.' His eyes drifted over her again. 'Please tell me you at least have panties on underneath.'

Her skin felt hot under his eyes. 'You ripped them.' Right about the time he'd fallen to his knees.

He stilled and she knew he was remembering the same

thing that she was. 'So I did.' He drew her into the circle of his arms. 'How are you feeling this morning?'

Embarrassed. Confused. *Wanton*… 'Good,' she said gruffly, unsure what the post-sex etiquette was with a man who was still a virtual stranger to her.

'You're not sore?' His eyes scanned hers. 'I wasn't exactly as gentle as I had promised for your first time.'

Farah knew she was blushing and hated the way he so effortlessly undermined her self-possession while he remained so composed. It hardly seemed fair. 'Not sore at all,' she lied blithely. If he was unaffected by her, then she was equally unaffected by him.

About to pull away and ask for a coffee, she gasped as his hands skimmed up her waist and cupped her breasts. Her eyes flew to his as her hands manacled his wrists, her breathing uneven. 'Zach?'

He strummed his thumbs across her nipples. 'How about here? Was I too rough here?'

He knew he hadn't been. He knew right now she was so turned on she was about to melt at his feet. 'I… I… What about your finger?'

He lifted her onto the bench and stepped between her legs. 'My finger is not the part of my anatomy that is concerning me at the moment.' He tugged at the zip on his jeans, his eyes on her mouth. 'Something else is.'

Farah's insides clenched hungrily as that something else sprang thick and long from the opening in his jeans. She licked her lips and did what she had wanted to do ever since she'd felt him against her: she reached out and touched him, circling him with her fist.

He groaned and gripped the bench either side of her hips, tension drawing the skin on his face tight. Forgetting all about how awkward and confused he made her feel, she moved her hand experimentally along his smooth, solid length, loving the loss of composure she saw in his expression.

'Firmer,' he rasped, his head bowed back, the muscles in his neck straining.

'Like this?' She stroked him again. Harder.

His nostrils flared as he brought heavy-lidded eyes back to hers. 'Oh yeah, just like that.'

Not giving herself time to think, Farah bobbed her head and took the tip of him into her mouth. The sound he made was deep and guttural, and his hands came up to cup the back of her head. The taste of him was hot and male on her tongue and a rush of liquid heat pooled between her thighs.

'Enough.' Zach urged her head up and yanked his T-shirt over her head, pushing her back on the bench and following her down to clamp his mouth over hers. He pushed her legs wide, his finger sliding inside her, and he groaned again. 'So wet, so ready, *habiba*.' And then he was there, sliding her forward off the bench and onto him.

Five minutes later, Farah was a sweaty mess on the bed with a heavy male panting on top of her.

'Farah, hell…' He raked a hand through his hair and levered himself off her. 'I was at least planning to feed you first.' Her stomach grumbled and he rolled her over so that she was on top of him. 'Sorry, sweetheart.'

'It's okay. It was…'

'Good?'

'Yes.'

'Shockingly good?'

'Yes.' She sighed, trying not to think too hard about anything. 'Is sex always like this?'

'It's called making love and, no, it's not.'

Making love? 'Ah, Zachim?' She wrinkled her nose as she smelt something burning.

He stroked his hand down the curve of her spine. 'Mmm?'

'Did you turn the stove off?'

'Holy—' Unconcerned about his nakedness, he vaulted from the bed and ran to the other room.

Grabbing his T-shirt again, she quickly donned it and followed, to find him rinsing a steaming pan under a tap, the inside charred to black.

He looked over his shoulder at her. 'I hope you like your bacon well-done.'

She laughed.

Later, they finally ate, and not a minute too soon, because Zach was sure his stomach had been about to feed on itself while he fed on her.

He looked across at her curled in the window seat, nursing a fresh cup of coffee and a faraway look as she gazed out over the tranquil blue waters of Talamanca Bay. The remains of their breakfast—eggs *sans* bacon—were pushed away on the breakfast table between them.

The air was balmy with late morning, the waters calm, and his thoughts somehow just as peaceful. The restless emptiness he'd been experiencing a few weeks ago strangely settled. *By this woman?*

The question threw him a little because he had no idea how she felt about him.

It was a surprisingly angst-ridden thought for a man who was used to women who would watch paint dry if he told them he found it fascinating. Not that Farah would. She'd no doubt roll her eyes and tell him a camel had more brains than he did. The thought made him smile and he was determined to remove the pensive look on her face.

Feeling strangely bereft of the skills that had led him arrogantly to claim that he was good with women and horses, he cleared his throat. 'You look troubled, *habiba*. Want to share?'

She glanced at him, her eyes guarded. Slowly she set her mug down on the table. 'It's nothing.'

He cocked an eyebrow and waited, resisting the need to haul her into his lap to comfort her and pet her. '*Nothing* seems to get us into trouble. How about we try some other word?'

A faint smile tugged at her lips. 'Okay, I was... I was thinking that we don't really know each other very well.'

'Well, we do,' he corrected lazily. 'But that's not what you meant.'

Her smile turned wry. 'No.'

'Okay, well, I know that you take your coffee white with one and you know I have mine black. What else would you like to know?'

'I don't know.' She made a face. 'What is your favourite breakfast?'

'Bacon,' he delivered, deadpan. 'Yours?'

She laughed and he took it as a small victory. 'Eggs with sumac, hummus on flatbread, yoghurt and dates.'

'What about toast with Vegemite?'

She frowned. 'What is that?'

'It's something I discovered on a tour of Australia. You will love it.'

She rolled her eyes. 'Naturally.'

He smiled. 'Favourite colour?'

'Too many to choose. You?'

He looked at her hair. 'Chestnut brown.'

She blushed beautifully. 'Favourite pastime?'

'Tinkering with engines. Yours?'

'Reading.'

Zach smiled as he felt some of the tension ease out of her. 'See? Already the marriage is working.'

'What about love?'

He stilled, his heart hammering. Was she about to tell him that love was important to her? That she didn't love him? 'What about it?' he asked gruffly.

'Your mother said you always wanted to marry for love.'

'My mother talks too much. Tell me how you came to use a sword so well.'

It was an obvious change of subject but Farah let it go because for some reason talking about love bothered her as much as it seemed to bother him. 'How *is* your arm?' she asked. 'I noticed this morning it still had a mark. I'm sorry I sliced you.'

'It was more of a nick, but I'm sorry I underestimated you. You're very good.'

She pulled a face. 'Hardly.'

He leaned over and tapped the edge of her nose. 'It was a compliment. So, what made you learn?'

That slight, vulnerable look he'd seen before briefly crossed her face and he was almost sorry he'd asked. Then she shrugged as if it didn't matter and he knew that it did. A lot.

'When my mother and unborn brother died my father was devastated and nothing I did seemed to help. One day while I was weaving a basket to sell at the markets, I saw how much fun the boys were having and how strong they looked, sparring with each other. It made me hate being a weak girl, so I asked to join them.'

'I'm surprised your father let you.'

'He didn't know.' She gave a rueful grimace. 'For a long time he was sort of absent. But I knew how badly he had wanted a son and I wanted to impress him. So I trained hard and entered the tournament that we hold at the village once a year—and I nearly won.'

He smiled. 'I have no doubt. And was he impressed?'

Farah looked across at Zach and realised just how much she'd told him and how easy he was to talk to—something else she hadn't expected. Deciding that she might as well continue, she hugged her knees into her chest. '*Shocked* is probably more the word I would use.' She pulled a rueful face, trying not to recall her father's harsh disapproval and her utter sense of hopelessness at the time. 'Sometimes it felt like nothing I did was—' She stopped, feeling more exposed than when she was lying before him naked.

'Good enough?' He filled in. 'Don't look so surprised, *habiba*. Your father isn't the only man to doll out conditional love.' His expression grew grim. 'My father was of the same ilk.'

Conditional love? Farah had never thought of it like that. Was that what her father gave? It seemed so obvious now, but always, in the past, she had thought there was something lacking in her.

A feeling of lightness came over her and she laughed. 'Why did I never think of that?'

Zach shrugged. 'Our fathers had a way of making us feel otherwise.'

Realising that Zach's father must not have approved of him, either, she leant forward. 'Are you saying you didn't see eye to eye with your father, either?'

Zach gave a short bark of laughter. 'That's putting it mildly. Nadir was always his favourite and he had little time for me as his *spare*.'

Farah heard the layer of pain behind that one word and her heart went out to him, not for one minute having thought that they would have something like this in common. 'And you never resented your brother for that?' Because at times she still felt guilty about her old feelings of resentment towards her unborn brother, certain that her own death would not have wrought half the pain in her father that his had.

'It wasn't Nadir's fault. My father was raised hard and he raised us hard.'

'Still, I admire that you didn't feel second-best.'

'Oh, I felt it. Often. Second-best. Third-best. I did everything to get his attention: being good, being bad, being funny, being smart, being strong... Then I realised that beating my head against a brick wall was only denting my head, not his, so I stopped. I joined the Foreign Legion, did a degree in engineering and started my own company. When I first got back to Bakaan—as you know—there was a lot to do to settle down the unrest. Then I saw how badly things had become and I did what I could behind the scenes.'

Did what he could? Farah blinked. 'It's you,' she said abruptly, instinctively knowing that he was the one who had organised the contraband goods their village—and probably others—received on a regular basis.

He smiled. 'I hope so.'

'No.' She shook her head, still dazed to think it might be true. 'You're the one who organised the medical supplies and educational material that is sent out to the villages in our area.'

He shrugged. 'I know it wasn't much, but it was all I could do while my father was alive. That will change though.'

'Thank you. That was…' She swallowed, struggling for words. For years she'd carried around a grudge against the Darkhans because she had blamed them for the loss of her mother and the happy life she had known before. She hadn't questioned the who, what or why of what had happened but had accepted her father's view and taken it on as her own. How could she have been so narrow-minded? How could she have let the past colour her view of the world so completely? 'I'm sorry. I think it was me who underestimated you this time.'

'Come here. I want to hold you.'

She unfolded shaky legs out from under her and went to him. She let him pull her down onto his lap and opened for him when he kissed her.

'You know, ever since you told me you were responsible for that publication five years ago I've been thinking about something.'

'What?'

'I want to suggest to Nadir that you become the ambassador for change in the outer regions.'

'What?' she parroted, unable to take in what he'd just offered.

'You have a sharp mind, *habiba*. It would be remiss of me not to utilise that. And changing years of cultural norms is not going to be easy. People will resist. They need to feel there is someone they can trust, especially since I am certain Nadir and I will be viewed sceptically at first.'

Farah chewed on the inside of her lip, her heart thumping hard at the thought. What he said made sense, and she would love it, but... 'You would let your wife work?'

'As long as it doesn't interfere with her home duties, of course.'

She felt her tentative bubble of hope burst. *Here it comes*, she thought, *the proviso*. She raised her chin. 'Such as?'

'Such as keeping our apartment spic and span, making sure my clothing is cleaned and ironed, servicing me whenever and wherever I— Oof!'

Farah punched him lightly on the shoulder, realising he was teasing her, and completely thrown by the unexpected playfulness. 'You're joking.'

He laughed deeply. 'For a non-violent person, you pack quite a punch.'

'I am usually non-violent,' she cried. 'I don't know what gets into me around you.'

The look he gave her could have heated the polar ice caps. 'I can tell you what gets into you.' His hands grew possessive, demanding. 'Me. And I have to tell you that every time you get feisty it makes me hot.'

Farah swallowed, instant arousal turning her limbs to jelly. 'Every time?'

As if knowing just how ready she was for him, he drew

in a sharp breath and rose, with her still in his arms as if she were no heavier than one of the cushions they'd been seated on.

'Every time.' He strode inside and dumped her on the sofa, his hands raising her T-shirt and sliding along the sensitive skin of her belly. 'But I was serious about one of those duties.' He fingered his belt buckle. 'Want me to demonstrate?'

Feeling herself melting, and unable to contain it, she reached up and pulled him down over her. 'Maybe a little more instruction might be worthwhile.'

CHAPTER TWELVE

IT WAS SOME sort of loud banging that roused Zach from a sweet dream and a deep sleep. Thinking it was an alarm, he rolled over and thumped the digital clock on the bedside table. Farah stirred beside him and he automatically tightened his arm around her shoulders.

She settled deeper into the crook of his arm and he closed his eyes.

Before arriving in Ibiza, while Farah had slept on the plane, Zach had made some plans about what they would do after they had settled in. First they would explore the beaches around Talamanca Bay, then they'd fly to a little out-of-the-way Spanish restaurant he knew in Dalt Vila, maybe sail around the beautiful island of Es Vedra and watch the sunset from the popular spot nearby.

What they ended up doing was never leaving the apartment—three days in and out of bed eating takeout that was brought by his security detail and introducing Farah to trashy TV—to which his new wife was now addicted. His mouth quirked at her penchant for Doris Day movies and he made a mental note to check the guide before channel-surfing with her again. He'd tried to explain that real men didn't watch romantic movies but she'd nestled more comfortably against him and he'd shut up. And enjoyed himself.

He'd also enjoyed breakfast. Since learning what she

preferred, he'd had the food stockpiled and he liked to watch her potter around, fixing share plates for them both while he brewed the coffee. Then he'd pop the toast in the toaster and over their meal he'd try to convince her to give Vegemite a go. So far she'd steadfastly refused but he'd seen the look of horror cross her face when she'd dipped her little finger in the jar to test it. He'd nearly laughed out loud but instead had kissed her into a stupor before bending her over the table and lifting her—his—T-shirt.

Damn, but he loved her in his T-shirts, with all that dark hair rippling down her back, her feet bare. All in all he'd say she fascinated him and in a surprisingly short space of time, his feelings for his wife had deepened to the point that he now struggled to label them. In fact if he didn't know better he'd think— The loud thumping started up again, breaking his train of thought.

'Darkhan, you lazy bastard,' a voice hollered from downstairs. 'We know you're in there. Your security team told us.'

Farah stiffened in his arms. 'Who is that?'

'Shh,' he murmured as he disentangled himself from her limbs. 'I'll take care of it.'

He grabbed his jeans on the way out and shoved them on. Then he headed downstairs and opened the front door of the villa. Sunlight spilled over the terracotta-tiled portico. Damian and Luke stood there, grinning like tomcats.

'You idiots ever heard of calling first?' Zach complained.

'We did. We've been calling and texting since yesterday.' Damian pushed past him into the foyer. 'You didn't respond.' He slapped him on the back. 'It's great to see you.'

'I forgot to check my phone.' In fact he hadn't checked his phone since...well, he couldn't remember.

Luke ambled past at a slower pace. 'Sweet digs. We

thought you might be side-tracked by a beautiful...' His friend's voice trailed off and Zach followed his gaze to the top of the stairs where Farah stood in nothing but his T-shirt, holding a large chef's knife in her hand. Zach grimaced. He really needed to show her where the suitcases were. And as for the knife... She squeaked out a noise as she noticed the three of them taking in her long legs and darted out of sight.

'Woman,' Damian filled in as Luke still stared wide-eyed. 'And you are!'

'Was that a knife?' Luke asked, confused.

'Ah, a fake one,' Zach parried. 'And she's not just any woman. She's my wife.'

He heard the note of pride in his voice and wondered if his friends did, too, the feeling he was struggling to name swelling inside his chest.

'*Wife?* Well...hell,' Damian sputtered. 'I thought I heard hearts breaking when I woke up this morning. Where was the invite?'

'We kept it small.'

'So, okay...' Luke shook his head as if he couldn't quite believe it. 'So, when you coming to the dock?'

'I don't know. I'll have to check with Farah.'

His two friends exchanged glances.

'You're coming to my party tonight, though, right?' Damian questioned. 'I mean, that is why you're here, isn't it?'

'If the missus says yes,' Luke said with mock seriousness.

'Well, of course,' Damian agreed. 'If the missus says—'

'All right, all right,' Zach growled, half wondering if Damian's party was really a good idea. 'You two morons have had your fun, now shove off or you can forget a present.'

'As long as she's long-legged and big—'

Zach slammed the door on their laughing faces. His

friends were confirmed bachelors and Zach was just glad not to be one of them any more.

He took the stairs two at a time and found Farah sitting cross-legged on the bed. He glanced around. 'Where's the knife?'

'In the kitchen.'

He made a mock-salute to the ceiling and saw her mouth twitch. 'Feel like a walk to the harbour?'

Her face brightened. 'Yes. I'd love it. But I haven't a thing to wear.'

Zach strolled to the walk-in closet, opened the suitcase and pulled out a pair of tiny shorts. He'd told her maid to pack the Western clothing Imogen had organised for him, but he'd yet to show Farah. He grabbed a white T-shirt he knew would show off her olive skin and dark hair to perfection, lace panties and a bra he couldn't wait to remove.

She frowned when he dropped them on the bed. 'Where did these come from?'

'The built-in 'robe.'

'The…' she frowned. 'I thought they were your suitcases in there. Why didn't you tell me?'

'You didn't ask.' He smiled. 'And it wasn't as if you needed clothing.'

'Oh.' Clearly embarrassed, she picked up the shorts. 'What are these?'

'Shorts.'

She eyed them sceptically. 'And what do I wear them with?'

'A T-shirt. Flip-flops.'

'Flip-flops?'

'Footwear.'

She held the shorts against her hips and glanced back at him. 'What else do I wear on my legs?'

'Ah, nothing.'

She frowned. 'On the street?'

'Sure.'

She shook her head. 'No.' She jumped up off the bed and inspected the closet. A century later she came out holding a pair of jeans. 'Where are my usual clothes?'

'I thought you'd be more comfortable in Western clothing.'

Her mouth pinched together and, just as he readied himself for an argument, she surprised him and huffed out a breath. 'I'll try them.'

Thinking the day couldn't get any better, he nearly choked when she came out after her shower dressed in the T-shirt and jeans. She pulled at the denim but they just sprung back into place, hugging her toned thighs as if they were sprayed on. 'These don't fit.'

Zach nodded. 'Turn around.'

She did a quick twirl and he frowned. 'You've just given me another idea,' he said.

'What?'

'I'm going to tell Nadir to make the wearing of jeans mandatory for all women in Bakaan, stat.'

She rolled her eyes and put her hands on her hips and a shaft of sweet pleasure shot straight to Zach's heart. 'Be serious,' she chided.

'I am.' He strolled towards her and curled his fingers into the waistband of her jeans, wondering if he'd ever felt happier than he did right now. 'Very serious about making love to my wife one more time.'

Farah couldn't stop smiling as they stepped out of the villa and into the bright sunshine. She hadn't expected to feel this…this light-hearted about being married; this light-hearted about the man she was married to. She snuck a quick glance at him and tried not to ogle him in his fitted T-shirt, denims and tapered sunglasses.

When he took her hand her heart seemed to skip a beat

and she focused on her surroundings to tamp down the emotions she instinctively knew she had to keep in check.

The harbour town was totally beautiful with its aqua-blue bay, sandy beaches and rows of pastel-coloured high-rise apartments and villas set into the hillside.

But it was the people who held most of her attention, old and young and dressed in every combination of cloth-ing she had ever seen in her magazines. One woman even had a small dog in her handbag with a diamond-studded collar and a bow in its hair. And then there was the trio of eye-catching women promenading towards them. They were slender to the point of being skinny, tanned golden-brown and wearing... She frowned, unable to recall what the word was for what looked like underwear. And they were looking at Zach as if they wanted to eat him alive.

'Careful, *habiba*, you're about to cut off my circulation.'

'I'm sorry.' Farah instantly eased her grip on his hand. 'I just... Those women aren't wearing any clothes.'

Zach chuckled. 'They're wearing bikinis. Swimwear,' he elaborated when she looked at him blankly.

'They're positively indecent,' she whispered.

'Sexy,' he corrected.

'You think they're sexy?'

His eyes skated over her body. 'Sure. On the right woman.'

Before she could ask who the right woman was, he re-directed her. 'Down here.'

Farah continued to be bug-eyed as Zach led her along a beautiful pier lined with yachts the size of tall buildings. At the end was a row of streamlined boats, much smaller and shaped like brightly coloured race cars without wheels. Men were scurrying around them and, combined with the sound of the engines revving and the smell of petrol, the air was alive with a sense of expectation and fun. More girls in bikinis lined the pier, leaning over the weathered railing like decorations.

Sticking close to Zach, Farah feigned a nonchalance she was far from feeling while he introduced her to his two friends from earlier and a group of other men and women who were clearly enamoured by the prince.

When one of the men suggested Zach take the boat for a test run, she saw his face light up. 'And I thought I was going to have to pull the owner card to get the gig.'

Owner? He owned the boats?

Turning to her, he checked if she was okay and she nodded. No way was she going to let him know that she was feeling completely out of her depth and wishing they were back in the apartment. Back in bed.

It was only when the shiny speedboat revved away from the pier and took off in a powerful arc of white water that she felt riveted to the spot.

'Watch how fast he is.' Luke came up beside her. 'There's no one better behind the wheel.'

Farah watched and her heart flew into her mouth when the bullet-shaped boat became airborne before crashing back down, spraying water into the air. 'Is it supposed to do that?'

'Oh yeah.' His friend didn't bother to hide his admiration. 'I wouldn't be surprised if he wants to race again sometime.'

'Race?'

'Yeah, he was unbeatable once, and when he left he said his stint was over and he'd never get back in one of those babies again. But then he said he'd never marry a Bakaani girl, either.' He winked at her. 'Never say never, eh?'

Never marry a Bakaani girl?

Before she could fully process that piece of information, Zach had pulled the boat up to the pier and men were yelling and readying themselves to hold it steady.

The look on his face was one of exhilaration and joy

and she felt a momentary pang that he would never look at her like that.

Brushing off her suddenly morbid thought, she nodded as Luke told her he'd see her at the party before jumping down to join Zach.

'Luke said you might race again,' she mentioned to Zach as they wandered back along the harbour a short time later.

'No.' Zach held her hand again. 'When I finished up, I meant it.' He stopped in front of an enormous navy-and-white yacht with music and lively conversation coming from the upper decks. 'Ready?'

No, she wasn't ready. She wanted to ask him about what Luke had told her but something warned her to hold off. What did it matter anyway? She knew he hadn't wanted to marry her. He'd made that plain.

She glanced up to find Zach looking at her curiously and wondered if he guessed how unsettled she felt. 'Sure,' she hedged, pride refusing to let her lean against him, as if she was the kind of woman who could not take care of herself.

Still, she couldn't seem to stem her unease once they boarded the yacht, and the curious glances she received as more and more people realised she was with the prince didn't help at all. The women especially gave her a weird vibe and didn't seem to know what to make of her once they'd asked where she was from and how she had met the prince. Farah kept her answers deliberately vague— 'My father introduced us'—which earned her a smile from Zach. After that most people either ignored her or saw someone in the distance they simply had to speak with and walked away.

Whatever.

Farah didn't care. For the most part Zach kept her by his side, proudly introducing her as his wife, and she was more pleased than she would have expected to be by that.

Especially given that this marriage had been forced on both of them. Somehow in the past three days that hadn't seemed relevant in the isolated nest of the apartment where she'd come to learn that, far from being an arrogant despot, her new husband was actually a kind and decent human being. But he still hadn't chosen to marry her out of free will, and probably never would have if his friend's unintentionally hurtful words were true.

'Having a good time?'

About to tell Zach she'd prefer to muck out the camel enclosure in her village, she turned her head to find him watching her with an expression on his face that melted her from the inside out. And suddenly she was determined that, yes, she would have a good time in this life he seemed to enjoy so much. 'Yes!' she said, turning her face up to his.

'I'm glad.' He leaned over and kissed her softly before drawing back with his arm slung around her waist. His possessive touch was comforting but, try as she might, she couldn't set aside the feeling of vulnerability that gripped her, surrounded as she was by so many glamorous people, especially those whispering behind their hands as they looked at her. Were they wondering what Zach was doing with her? Or did they all know that he had been forced to marry her? That given a choice he would have preferred any one of the beautiful women parading around on the yacht in their *sexy* triangles of material. Would Zach ever expect her to wear one of those, in public? If so, he was going to be incredibly disappointed, because that just wasn't her.

'Zach.'

Someone—a woman—said his name in a low, throaty murmur and Farah turned to find a slender, elegant blonde looking up at him. She was tiny and delicate and so flawlessly beautiful she was hard to look away from.

Used to having women come up to him by now, Farah

at first didn't pay her any special attention, but then she realised that Zach had grown tense.

'I heard you got married,' the woman said, casting Farah a brief glance.

'Yes.' Something in his tone made the hairs on the nape of Farah's neck stand on end. 'Amy, I'd like you to meet my wife, Farah.' His fingers flexed on her hip. 'Farah, this is Amy Anderson.'

Farah had wondered more than once who the woman was that Zach had nearly married and suddenly she knew she was standing right in front of her. It was obvious in every casually awkward line of the woman's body and the answering tension in her husband's.

The woman had a peaches-and-cream complexion Farah would never achieve even if she stayed out of the sun for a decade, and the way she was looking at Zach made it very clear that, if she could, she would trade places with Farah in a heartbeat. Feeling about as attractive as a desert shrub in a French garden, Farah smiled. 'I'm pleased to meet you.'

'And you,' Amy said with a warmth Farah wasn't sure reached her eyes.

'How long ago did you break up?' she asked a little dully as the beautiful Amy finally wandered off into the crowd.

Zach grimaced faintly. 'Was it that obvious?'

Farah felt old beyond her years. 'A woman knows these things.' Not that she ever would have thought she would.

'Five years ago.'

Five years ago? Farah frowned. Was that because he'd had to return to Bakaan? Had she inadvertently broken up his relationship when she had tried to implement change with her little magazine? It seemed impossible.

She wanted to ask if he had been in love with her but she knew that he must have been if he'd nearly married her. Did he still? The sick feeling she had experienced on her wedding day thinking about the exact same thing balled in her stomach, but there was no way she would ask him because she really didn't want to know the answer. In fact, she didn't want to *think* about the answer.

As if reading her every thought, he took her chin gently between his fingers to bring her eyes to his. 'If you're worried that I'll cheat on you, Farah, I won't. I'm not like that. Amy is in my past.'

Deep down she knew that he was telling the truth but it didn't change the fact that he had once wanted to marry Amy and he had never wanted to marry her—and why was she so fixated on that all of a sudden?

'I'm not worried, I—'

'Prince Zachim.' A large man in a cream suit that stretched across his ample belly and a matching Stetson stopped beside them, an overconfident smile on his face. 'Not interruptin', am I?'

'I've never known you *not* to interrupt, Hopkins,' Zach said mildly, making the man laugh.

'Always did enjoy your sense of humour, Your Highness. This is Cherry, my wife. And you must be Zach's new wife.'

'Farah,' Zach supplied grudgingly.

'Good to meet you, ma'am.' The man took her hand in that deferential manner men did when they were putting women in their place before dismissing her in favour of Zach. 'I was hoping to talk to you about building hotels over in that country of yours, Your Highness, and there's no time like the present.'

'Actually, there is. And now isn't it.'

'Oh, come now, we fly back to Dallas tomorrow. Cherry will take care of your little lady for a spell, won't you, sugar?'

'Of course!' the vivacious redhead exclaimed. 'I'd be glad to.'

'Some other time, Hopkins. Farah and I were just leaving.'

'It's okay, Zach.' Farah put her hand on his arm, knowing from an earlier conversation they'd had how important new investments were to Bakaan and not wanting to be the reason he missed an opportunity, even if the man was a bit of windbag. 'I'll be fine.'

'See? She'll be fine.' The man gave her an oily smile. 'You got to let 'em either sink or swim, don't you, sugar?'

The look on Zach's face told her he wanted to make this man sink or swim and it gave her the urge to giggle. Instead she moved away from him and murmured a greeting to the man's nubile wife who was spilling out of a red polka-dot bikini top above white jeans that looked tighter than her own.

Within minutes Farah found herself amidst a small knot of Cherry's chic friends, including the beautiful Amy, who all wanted the gossip on how she had landed the prince— gossip Farah had no intention of giving them because it would only show them how little she really meant to her husband!

'At least tell us if he's as hot in the sack as they say he is,' one of the women whispered.

'Tia! You can't ask that,' another woman admonished.

'Oh, don't pretend you're not dying to know, Pansy, you tried to get him yourself once without any success. I heard he was into threesomes, as well. Is that true?'

Threesomes? No way was Farah naively going to ask what that was.

'Tia, you're so naughty!' Pansy giggled and took Farah's arm. 'Please ignore our friend. She's had too much champagne and she's had some seriously bad dates.' She glanced down at Farah's empty hands. 'Oh, Lordy, you don't have a drink. Waiter, champagne, *por favor*!'

'I'm fine,' Farah quickly assured her. 'I was sick the last time I had champagne.'

'So?' Tia asked.

'Oh, you're adorable,' Pansy interjected as if Farah was a puppy she'd just won in a competition. 'Isn't she adorable?'

Amy cast her a cool smile and sipped her own champagne as if she had no trouble with the drink at all. 'How long have you and Zach known each other?'

Farah felt the woman's interest like the pointed end of a sword to her solar plexus. 'Not that long.'

'Was it a whirlwind courtship?' Cherry asked, sipping a red drink with a paper umbrella sticking out of the top.

Farah thought about her father ordering Zach to marry her. 'I guess you could call it that.'

'You must have something special going on under the hood,' Tia drawled knowingly. 'To keep the attention of man like that.'

'Have you seen the way he looks at her? H. O. T. Hot,' Pansy said. 'Oh, look, there's the girl I saw earlier with the goody bags. Yoo-hoo, over here.'

Feeling a small glow at Pansy's observation that Zach looked at her in some special way, Farah watched as a much younger woman in a tiny bikini sauntered over with a basket of small delicately fringed purses inside.

'What's in them?' Tia eyed the bags with bored interest. 'If it's not diamonds, I'm not interested.'

'Chocolates,' the woman said.

'Oh, definitely not, then.' She shuddered as if the woman had said snakes.

'I'll take one,' Cherry said, reaching into the bag. 'What about you, Panse? Amy?'

'Which is which?' Pansy eyed the three different-coloured purses.

'There's dark, white and a combination of the two.'

Pansy selected the combination. 'Farah?'

'Oh…' Farah scanned the small purses, suddenly re-

membering the other night when Zach had ordered straw-
berries and chocolate sauce and proceeded to eat most of
them. Off her. She couldn't prevent a small smile from
sneaking across her lips and her heartbeat quickened.
'Dark, please.'

'Really?' Amy stepped forward to eye the selection.
'I'd choose the white if I were you.' She rifled through the
purses as if hunting for the perfect specimen. 'Zach is more
a vanilla kind of guy.' She glanced up at Farah through a
veil of thick lashes. 'If you know what I mean.'

Farah blinked, wondering if she'd heard her right. When
she saw Pansy's wide-eyed stare and Tia's amused smirk,
she knew she hadn't misinterpreted the other woman's
subtle put-down. Heat rushed into her face, making her
insecurities spike. She bent over the basket, pride insisting
she choose the purse holding the dark treats. This woman
might be right about Zach's preferences, but he wasn't hers
any more, and Farah took some comfort from Zach's earlier reassurance that Amy was in his past.

'Maybe he's changed,' she said casually, attempting to
calm her galloping heartbeat. 'Five years is a long time.'

Amy's small smile could have frozen the sun. 'Five
years?' She cocked her head, as if confused. 'I meant last
week.'

Last week? Farah felt herself reel and couldn't stop the
barrage of questions from flooding her brain. *Had Zach
lied when he'd said Amy was in his past?* And what of
the tender consideration he'd given her over the past few
days? *Had that just been his way of making the best of a
bad situation?*

'Oh, look, there's Morgan O'Keefe,' Amy said. 'If you'll
excuse me?'

There was a short, loaded silence as they watched Amy
saunter across the crowded deck and then Pansy patted her

arm. 'Don't mind her,' she said. 'She was obviously looking to start a row.'

'She's jealous,' Tia said offhandedly. 'She was sure she
was the next Princess of Bakaan but it didn't come off.
Move on, I say.'

'Oh, right, like you've moved on from Gary?' Pansy
chortled.

'Do not mention that man around me,' Tia hissed, making the other two girls burst into peals of laughter.

Farah watched them, feeling as if she was listening
to them from afar, a sort of numbness working its way
through her system.

'Ready to go?'

Zach appeared at her side and Farah pinned a bright
smile on her face. 'Of course.'

CHAPTER THIRTEEN

'OKAY, OUT WITH IT,' Zach said, shutting the front door to the apartment and turning to face Farah.

She paused on the first step of the stairs. 'Out with what?'

He came towards her and shoved his hands in his pockets so that he didn't put them on her. Once they were there, her clothing was coming off, but he could tell there was something weighing on her mind that needed to be dealt with first. 'Whatever's bothering you.'

'There's nothing bothering me.'

She continued up the stairs and he followed, trying to keep his eyes off the sway of her bottom in those jeans. 'Pull the other one, it's got bells on it.'

'Sorry?'

Seeing her pained look, he sighed. 'It's just an expression.' He stopped her at the top of the stairs, his eyes searching hers. 'Talk to me,' he said softly. She smiled brightly as she had on the yacht and he wondered if she truly expected him to fall for it. 'Please,' he added.

'Okay…' Her throat worked as she swallowed. 'What's a threesome?'

'A what?' Zach nearly choked at the question. Now, *that* he hadn't been expecting. 'How— Who—' He shook his head. 'Why are you asking about threesomes?'

'One of the women said that you like them.'

'Ah, I see you've been listening to gossip.' His eyes searched hers but she kept her gaze averted, so he guessed that wasn't the real question on her mind, but damn...

He ran a hand through his hair before moving into the kitchen to pull a bottle of water from the fridge, pouring them both a glass. Really he should have just ditched the party when he'd first thought to. Ironic when the whole purpose of coming to Ibiza had been to see his friends and immerse himself in his old lifestyle, to get his spark back. Now all he wanted was to immerse himself in Farah. In fact it was all he could think about. Even when flying over the water in Damian's jet boat, at speeds that usually wiped all thought from his mind, he'd compared it to the joy of waking with her in his arms.

Not wanting to dwell on what that meant, he focused on explaining a threesome to her. 'Okay, well, first a three-some is sex with three people.' When she stared at him blankly, he continued. 'At the same time.'

'Oh.' She blinked. 'I figured it was something sexual but I thought perhaps it was three different positions or something.' She leaned her elbows on the counter top and absently ran a hand up and down the glass of water. 'Is it two men and a woman or two women and a man?'

Zach coughed into his hand. 'It can be either. Why? Are you interested?'

She raised limpid brown eyes to his and her nose wrin-kled. 'I've never thought about it before, but...not par-ticularly.'

He blew out a breath. 'Good because I don't share. Which should answer your question as to whether I'm into them or not. But, as interesting as that little diversion was, it wasn't the reason behind your quiet state.'

Surprise flickered in her eyes before she lowered them. 'How do you know that?'

'I have good instincts.'

'You mean you're cocky.'

'That, too.' He smiled to try and lighten the mood. 'Tell me I'm wrong.'

'You're wrong.'

'Farah!'

'Okay, fine. Did you see that woman Amy last week?'

Zach blinked. Hell he hadn't been expecting that one, either. 'No. I haven't seen Amy for five years. Why do you ask?'

'No reason.'

She moved into the living area and he followed. 'Farah, don't fob me off. Why did you ask?'

'She implied that you had...' She shrugged. 'But it was probably my mistake.'

Possibly. Or possibly Amy had wanted to cause trouble between them because she was upset that he hadn't shown any interest in catching up with her. She had definitely been put out to find him married and maybe that was his fault. 'Amy emailed me last week asking to catch up tonight,' he admitted.

Something he'd completely forgotten about until just now. In fact it had been a shock to see her at the party and even more of a shock to realise that he felt nothing for her. Maybe she'd picked up on that and also that he was completely enamoured with his new wife.

Was that how he felt about Farah? *Enamoured?*

Looking at her now, her bedroom eyes large in her face, her hair tumbling around her stiff shoulders, her curvy figure outlined to perfection... A sense of destiny whispered across the surface of his mind. The fact was he couldn't remember ever making outrageously arrogant statements to Amy or any other woman just to make her laugh because it lit something up inside him, nor had he wanted to watch her do the simple act of rubbing the sleep from her eyes in the morning, and he certainly hadn't wasted time on a TV program other than sports just because he'd wanted to hold her in his arms for a little longer.

'So you had arranged to see her?'

It took Zach a full minute to shift his focus from what his mind was trying to tell him to what Farah had asked. When he did, he grimaced. 'Yes, but that was before we married and as I said before, I have no intention of being unfaithful to you. You said you believed me.'

She moved over to the wall of windows and stared outside. 'I do.'

Zach sucked in a slow breath. He'd expected her to be happy at his declaration so he was beyond perturbed when she ignored him in favour of staring out at the darkness. Did that mean she didn't believe him?

'I can see the look of doubt on your face but I'm telling you the truth.' Amy really was in his past because, regardless of what happened between him and Farah, it had been obvious to Zach tonight that his brother had called it right about Amy years ago.

Wanting to eradicate the far away look on Farah's face, he slipped his hand down to hold hers, coming into contact with the silk purse he'd vaguely noticed on the drive to the apartment. 'What's this?'

She stared at it as if she didn't realise she was still holding it. 'Chocolates. They were giving them out at the party. Do you want one?'

No, he didn't want one. 'I want to know whether you believe that I will be faithful to you first.'

'I do.'

'Farah—'

'They're dark, though,' she said, holding up the chocolates as if that somehow made a difference. Personally Zach couldn't care if they were gold-coated and he frowned at the bag.

'You do like dark chocolate, don't you?'

He heard the tremor in her voice and sighed. 'I love dark chocolate.'

That made her lip tremble even more and yet again he found himself at a loss as to how to communicate with this woman. So he said nothing, just stared out at the dark bay beyond the window and waited.

'Dark, isn't it?'

Zach's eyebrows drew down. They were going to talk about the weather now? 'That it is.'

He tried to keep the impatience from his voice when he answered but he wasn't sure he'd succeeded when she stiffened.

'I could have chosen white chocolate instead.'

What the— 'Farah?' He turned her to face him and saw a glittering wetness in her eyes. If this was Amy's doing he'd throttle her. '*Habiba*, sweetheart… What's…?'

'Am I too dark for you?'

He shook his head. 'Too dark?'

'My skin, my hair, my eyes. I realised tonight that I've only ever seen you photographed with fair-haired women and Luke said you had never intended to marry a Bakaani woman. Is that why…? Is that…?'

Zach swore roughly. Perhaps he'd bury Luke and Amy together. 'Listen to me,' he ordered. 'I did say that once but I was young and stupid and rebelling against my father's expectations of me. I'm married to you now so none of that matters. It's in the past.'

Was it?

Farah desperately wanted to believe him, she really did, but it wasn't easy. How could he want her when she so obviously didn't fit his criteria of the ideal woman? And, oh, how she hated the feeling of insecurity that rose up inside her. The feeling that no matter how hard she tried she would never be good enough.

Placing her hands flat against the window, she spread her fingers out like starfish against the cool glass. The move gave her a sense of vertigo and she suddenly knew what was at the root of her current mood. She suddenly knew why it was so important that Zach hadn't chosen her and why Amy and Luke's comments had hurt so much. She suddenly understood that, even though she had guarded her heart so closely and for so long, she had done the foolish thing of falling in love with her husband.

She, who had imagined that such a thing would never happen to her. She, who had always believed that love and marriage limited a woman's chance at happiness—and still did. Bile collected at the base of her throat. How had she been so stupid?

'Farah.' Zach stepped in behind her and splayed his fingers over the top of hers, somehow anchoring her when what she wanted was to spin out into the ether and never come back. Holding her hips roughly, he pressed his groin against her bottom, his erection hard and unyielding through the denim of his jeans.

Sweet sensation swept through her and she couldn't prevent a small gasp from escaping her lips as instant heat and moisture collected at the juncture of her thighs.

'Does that feel like I think you're too dark?' he growled.

Confused and confounded by the depth of her feelings for this man, Farah didn't know what to say without revealing how she felt.

'Does it?' he repeated gruffly.

She shook her head. 'No. But you could be...you could be thinking of someone else.'

The growl turned rough and came from deep in his chest. One of his hands fisted in her hair and brought her eyes to his in the glass. Then he slid his other hand over her belly until it met the snap on her jeans. One flick and the button was released, followed by the zip, and then his hand was on her and in her, and Farah's head fell back against his shoulder as she surged between the firmness of his fingers in front of her and the ridge of his erection behind her.

'Yes,' he growled, the fingers of his other hand going beneath her T-shirt to rub across both her nipples at once. 'You're mine, Farah. All mine.'

Her climax built almost instantly and, just when she was reaching for it, he removed his fingers and worked her jeans down her hips.

'Not without me.' Within seconds he had his own jeans open and then he was there, bending her forward, her hands splayed once more on the glass, as he pushed into her in one powerful thrust. 'Look at me,' he demanded, surging hard. 'Look at me when I take you.' His eyes never left hers as he established a driving rhythm that left her in no doubt as to who was in control. 'Watch my face while I'm inside you. See for yourself that it's you who does this to me, it's you who makes me so damned out of control it sometimes scares me.'

He groaned as Farah pushed back and shattered in a shower of sensation, her body pulsing around his flesh and sucking him in deep. 'Hell, Farah.'

He spilled his release inside her and Farah collapsed limply against the glass, her only support the man breathing heavily at her back who had one arm wrapped around her middle and the other planted against the window.

He leaned forward and nuzzled the sweaty hair that stuck to the nape of neck. 'I didn't mean for that to happen. I'm sorry.'

'It's okay.'

'I've just wanted you all damned day and to hear you say what you did—' He stopped abruptly and adjusted his jeans before picking her up in his arms and carrying her across the room to their darkened bedroom.

He placed her on the bed and stripped off her clothing before switching on the bedside lamp, bathing them both in a golden glow. Then he stripped off his own and came over the top of her, all dominant and elementally male. Farah felt her heart kick behind her rib cage; she'd never seen him so wildly masculine before, so completely out of control.

Holding himself off her with the strength in his arms, he stared down at her. 'I want you to trust me, Farah.'

Trust him...

'I want you to rely on me.'

She didn't doubt she could on some level, but one day he would see that she wasn't enough for him and what then? 'Relying on others isn't easy for me. It's—'

'I'm not asking you to rely on *others*,' he said fiercely. 'I'm asking you to rely on *me*. I won't hurt you, Farah.' He rolled to the side and took her with him. 'In fact you need to know that, if you ever want to leave, you only have to say so.'

'Leave?' She was in such a confused state she wasn't sure that he wasn't asking her to leave.

He smoothed the hair back from her forehead. 'I mean, I won't chase you or force you to stay like my father would have done. Like he tried to do with Nadir's mother.' Farah had heard the story about Nadir's mother, who had been trying to leave the sheikh with her daughter and had died in a tragic car accident when he'd had them followed. 'If we can't make this marriage work, you are free to go.'

Farah's mouth suddenly felt dry. 'You really mean that?'

'Yes.'

'But how? Under Bakaani law a woman is not free to leave her husband.'

'Not yet she isn't. But that is another ancient law that is in the process of being changed.'

She stared up at him. 'And my father?'

'Your father goes free from this moment on.'

His words were a pledge that Farah knew he would keep and once again she felt overwhelmed by the depth of her emotions for this man. She buried her head against his shoulder knowing that there was nothing she could give him that equalled all that he could give her. All that he *had* given her.

She felt the brush of his lips against the top of her head and felt like weeping—she, who never cried.

'It's okay, my little Zenobia.' He sighed and gathered her closer. 'We'll return to Bakaan tomorrow and start our marriage properly. Everything will be good. You'll see.'

CHAPTER FOURTEEN

BUT TWO WEEKS later things weren't good, they were frustratingly bad, and Zach had no idea how to rectify the situation. Ever since their return from Ibiza, Farah had seemed to withdraw from him both physically and mentally and not even bringing her beloved stallion to the palace had made her happy.

He stared down at the list of law reforms he'd been sitting on for a week now. One of them was the new legislation giving women the right to apply to the courts for a divorce, the law he had promised Farah he would implement so that she could walk away from him if she wanted to.

Right now he had a feeling she'd do just that and he knew he didn't want that to happen. It was being so blasted busy that was getting in the way. Since they'd been back, they'd had to attend one state dinner after another as important world leaders came to Bakaan to discuss global issues and future strategies. Having pledged to help Nadir ride out the changes in Bakaan, Zach had done what was required of him and he had also kept his promise to include Farah. Which was both a boon and not, because she had taken to her role as regional ambassador so wholeheartedly that at this rate she could run the country singlehandedly by the end of next week. In fact, she worked so hard she'd often go to bed exhausted. So exhausted that lately he hadn't wanted to disturb her when he'd come to bed and let her sleep. Maybe that accounted for his sullen frame of mind—a build-up of sexual repression.

But he knew that wasn't it. He knew it was because he'd realised some time over the past couple of weeks he'd actually fallen in love with his wife and that she did not love him back. And, even worse, he couldn't help but wonder if her withdrawn state was because she had got what she wanted from him when he'd promised that he would not prosecute her father if they should divorce. Perhaps all she was waiting for was for the divorce laws to be changed and then she'd make her move.

Frustrated and agitated, Zach pushed back from his desk and strode to the window. His office overlooked the stables and his eyes immediately zeroed in on Farah, standing in the sunshine brushing down her stallion's sweaty coat.

The damned horse got more of her attention than he did and he now regretted bringing it to the palace. He'd done it a week ago to surprise her. He'd wanted to lift her spirits and show her how he felt, how much he appreciated her, and—he could admit now—he'd wanted her to tell him that she loved him, or at least cared for him—but she hadn't.

She'd wrapped her arms around the blasted horse's neck and told him she loved him instead. And the damned thing had looked like it would lie down and die for her.

Rubbing at the persistent tension at the back of his neck, Zach wondered what to do about his marriage. Logically he knew that he should just let her go—if that was indeed what she wanted—but he knew he hadn't offered her that so far because he wasn't sure that he could. Even now some deep-seated part of himself that must surely date back to his barbarian ancestors warned him that he couldn't.

It was almost laughable to think that he had once prided himself on how emotionally grounded he was when the truth was that right now he felt about as emotionally grounded as a log. He, who had fought in war zones, who had raced boats at over two-hundred miles per hour, and who had started up his own company without any financial backing was afraid to tell his wife how he felt.

Pathetic.

He watched her lead Moonbeam into the stable, her curvy bottom outlined to perfection in her jodhpurs. A grim smile came to his lips.

It was time he stopped pussyfooting around the edges of this marriage and confronted her head-on. If she happened to throw herself at him, and make love to him in the stables as a result, all the better. If she wanted out, well… hell, he'd give her that, too.

As Farah housed Moonbeam for the night she couldn't help but remember the day Zach had brought her beloved horse to her.

'Is the blindfold really necessary?' she'd asked nervously.

'Yes.'

She sniffed the air. 'We're in the stables.'

'Correct.'

Then he'd removed the blindfold and she'd stared at her white stallion, completely mute. When she'd found her voice, it was to whisper, 'What? How?'

'I had him brought here for you.'

'Oh, I love you,' she'd blurted out, throwing her arms around Moonbeam's neck, when she'd noticed the frown on Zach's face. She'd repeated the words over and over as if she'd been talking to the horse all along, but of course she hadn't, and it had nearly been one of the most singularly embarrassing moments of her life.

Even so, she'd ached to have Zach take her in his arms,

but he'd become even more remote and told her he'd leave her and Moonbeam to get reacquainted.

It had been like that a lot lately—Zach leaving her alone to do her work while he took meetings. Zach leaving her alone to have breakfast while he pounded out a circuit on his treadmill. Zach coming to bed late and then hardly touching her...

Farah felt a lump form in her throat. She knew he was busy and she had no wish to change that but what she'd love to change was the way he seemed to hold part of himself back from her. It was as if he was already regretting their marriage, and she couldn't help but wonder if their trip to Ibiza hadn't triggered a realisation in him that he had been seriously short-changed in being forced to marry her.

Oh, he had tried to reassure her that that wasn't the case, but what else could he have said? That, yes, he did regret it and would now risk inciting a war for his own selfish ends?

Once she would have believed him capable of such a thing. She knew that was no longer true. She knew that honour and integrity was the most important thing to him. As it was to her.

But at the expense of his happiness? Of her own?

With her head aching, she positioned Moonbeam's chaff bucket and leant her forehead against his shoulder as he ate. Lost as she was in thought, she didn't immediately hear anyone come up behind her.

'Farah?'

Whirling around at the sound of her name, she stared dumbfounded as Amir stood in the doorway to Moonbeam's stall with one of her private security detail as escort.

'Amir!'

'I hope this is not an intrusion, Your Highness,' her guard said. 'The palace staff said you were here and Mr Dawad was very insistent.'

'It's fine. Thank you.'

Bowing low, the guard left, and Farah stared at Amir, only then realising how much she really missed being around the familiar faces of her village.

'Is it my father? Has something happened?'

Amir walked towards her. 'No, he's good, although he is concerned about you. I think he regrets pushing you into this marriage.'

'Oh.' He and her both, she thought tiredly.

'He would like to know if you are happy. As we all would.'

'Amir...'

'Before you say anything, I would also like to apologise for my behaviour prior to all this blowing up. I was pushing you because I'm in love with you but that was wrong.'

Farah let out a slow breath. 'Oh, Amir, I... I didn't realise.' She had assumed he had only been trying to cement his place as the future leader of Al-Hajjar.

He gave her a faint smile. 'I know. So are you happy, Farah? Because if you're not I could take you away from all this.'

Farah closed her eyes against his words. She longed to be able to tell him outright that she was not only happy but positively joyous, that she had never been happier, but she wasn't and she had never been able to lie. And his declaration of love made her feel truly awful. It struck deep in her heart because she knew how unrequited love felt and it was debilitating. Every bit as debilitating as she had known love would be and there was no satisfaction in being proved correct.

'I'm not unhappy,' she hedged. Not a lie exactly. It wasn't unhappiness she felt, just a bone-deep sadness that Zach would never return her feelings.

'That's not good enough, Farah. That's a cop-out.'

He reached for her hands but before he could touch her a furious voice made them both jump.

'Who the hell let you inside the palace?'

Jumping almost sky high, Farah turned to face her husband.

'Greetings, Your Highness.'

She threw Amir a dark look to let him know that she did not appreciate his silky tone. 'Zach, Amir was—'

Zach shook his head at her. 'I'm asking him, not you.'

Brought up short by the reprimand, Farah blinked.

'I asked what you're doing here?'

Amir squared his shoulders, although the faint tremor that ran through him slightly mitigated any authority he tried to establish with the move. 'I've come to visit with Farah. Or is that not allowed?'

'No, it is not allowed.' Fury emanated from every tense muscle in Zach's body.

'Zachim—'

'It's fine, Farah.' Amir did not take his eyes off the prince. 'I can go.'

'Yes, you can,' Zach snarled, his eyes alight with murderous intent as Amir paused beside him and whispered something under his breath.

Farah couldn't hear what it was but it only made her husband's eyes turn colder. He raised his hand and security was there in an instant to do his bidding.

Mortified at the way he had just treated Amir who had only been trying to make amends Farah stared at him. 'Why did you treat my friend like that?'

'Why did he come into my home unannounced?'

'*Your* home?'

'Don't play semantic games with me, Farah. What did he want with you?'

'He wanted to make amends.'

Zach made a scathing noise in the back of his throat. 'He is not welcome here.'

Affronted by his easy dismissal of her wishes Farah bristled. 'He *is* welcome here.'

Blowing out a breath he stopped in front of her. 'I did not come here to argue with you.'

'Then stop being such an egomaniac,' she bit out, trying to keep the hurt from her voice. 'If I want to entertain a friend, then I will.'

Feet planted wide apart, he glowered at her. 'Not if I forbid it.'

'Not if you…?' All the confusing, unsettling emotions she'd been feeling ever since they'd returned to Bakaan coalesced into anger. Anger at herself, at him, anger at their whole, damned miserable arrangement. 'Don't you dare try and dictate what I can and can't do. I'm not your possession.'

She didn't have time to say anything else because Zach was on her, his mouth crashing down over hers in a demanding, controlling kiss that left her in no doubt just what he could and couldn't do. 'Yes, you are. You're mine, Farah. Don't ever forget it.'

His! Of all the… Forgetting her non-violence policy Farah lashed out at him, welcoming the spurt of adrenaline that came with a good fight.

Within seconds, however, he'd subdued her. 'Temper, temper, my little wild cat.'

'Oh.' Farah tossed her hair out of her face. 'You great, big, patronising—'

She didn't get any further because Zach's mouth covered hers again, his tongue duelling with her own and, oh, it felt so good to be held by him like this, so good to be kissing him with all the pent-up passion she'd been unable to express.

Moaning, she arched into him, melting against him as

he hitched her thigh up over his hip, angling his body into hers so that she was in no doubt as to how aroused he was. 'You are mine,' he breathed against her mouth. 'And if I don't want you to see someone because I deem it unsafe, then you won't.'

Incensed by his words, by her own traitorous body, Farah shoved against him, only coming up against the horse stall for her efforts. 'I can protect myself if that's what you're worried about,' she panted.

'Like now?'

He forced her hard up against the brick wall, his thigh wedged between her own in a move reminiscent of when he had trapped her in the alleyway.

Moonbeam shifted restlessly behind him, disturbed by all the pent-up emotion circulating in the room. A feeling of utter helplessness came over Farah and the weight of despair descended on her shoulders. Any hopes she had been harbouring that Zach cared for her, that he might one day want her with him because he respected her as his equal, dissolved into nothing. 'I hate you,' she said, unsure if it was him she hated or just herself for loving someone who did not love her in return.

'I don't give a damn.' He released her and swiped his hand across his mouth as if to wipe her taste away.

He didn't give a damn how she felt? 'Nice to know,' she said, before turning with as much dignity as she could muster and walking away from him.

Zach watched as she slowly walked away from him and nearly put his fist through the wall.

Where had all that anger come from? He hardly recognised himself. He, the king of communication, had just acted like Cro-Magnon man with an obsession.

Just thinking about it brought him out in a cold sweat. Usually he was great with women—even-tempered, patient, *considerate*. Just then he'd been…he'd been… Well, he hadn't handled himself at all well. He could admit that.

It had been the confident expression on Amir's face and his snide, 'I knew you wouldn't be able to make her happy,' as he'd walked past him that had done it.

Zach hated to admit it, but he'd got the better of him, because it had struck too close to the bone. And the whole time afterwards he'd been wondering what Farah had told him. What she had revealed to make the soldier so sure of himself.

I hate you.

'Great going, Darkhan. Maybe you can develop an app that will show men how to get their wives on side.'

Not.

He stopped pacing when he reached the back of the stable and clasped his hands over his head, trying to re-assemble his thoughts. One of the junior staff members caught sight of him and quickly scurried for cover.

First, he listed mentally, *you might hate the guy but you can't dictate who she does and doesn't see. You know that.*

Second, you need to pull back. Get some perspective on how this marriage is going to work.

And third… Third, he just needed to apologise to her for being such an idiot.

Feeling that his emotions were on simmer instead of a rapid boil, he took a deep breath and went in search of her.

When he found her in their living room reading a work file, it pulled him up short. Nice to know their argument hadn't interrupted *her* focus.

Glancing up as he approached, her eyes turned wary. He stopped and took a deep breath. 'I was wrong to yell at you. I'm sorry.'

'It doesn't matter,' she dismissed politely.

'Of course it matters,' he said just as politely.

'Look, Zach…' She hesitated. 'Things haven't really

been the same since we returned from Ibiza and if we're honest—' she took a breath '—which I like to think that we always have been with each other, then I can't see things getting any better between us.' She looked up at him then. 'Can you?'

Zach nodded as if he agreed but really he was thinking that he'd been right to assume that she wanted out of the marriage. She did but she was hardly being honest about it.

'The truth is,' she continued, 'we're both victims in this situation.'

Victims? 'You're only a victim if you think you're a victim,' he bit out tautly. 'And I am no victim.'

'Well, that's easy for you to say. You're a man and a prince.'

'I don't care what I am.'

'Fine.' She sighed heavily. 'I was only trying to make this easier.'

Zach paced across the room to put some distance between them. 'You were trying to say that now that I won't prosecute your father there's no reason for us to stay married. How's that for honesty?'

She flashed him a pained look. 'That's not the only reason but with the past laid to rest it certainly means that there's nothing holding us together any more.'

Nothing. There was that word again.

Zach looked at her and saw her eyes shiny with tears. Or was it defiance? Because she had done nothing but defy him all along and he...he'd been arrogant enough to assume that she would eventually fall for him as almost every other woman had. That he could make this marriage work from sheer will alone.

The truth was he hadn't wanted to disappoint his mother, who had suffered so many disappointments in her life, and he hadn't wanted to disappoint himself. But when you broke it down, he'd enjoyed the sex—a little too much in retrospect—and he'd done what a lot of women he'd been with had done with him: he'd mistaken lust for love.

'Zach?'

Talk about feeling like a chump.

He turned back to her. 'That's fine,' he heard himself saying as if he were an actor on set. 'I can see you've thought this through and, really, I've been so busy I haven't. But you're right. We have nothing holding us together.'

Shaken by Zach's ready acceptance of everything she'd said, Farah got up and restlessly moved around the room. She noticed that the orchid bloom, the gift from his mother, had fallen from its stem and laid on the table. Carefully she picked it up and cradled it in her palm, gently stroking the dying petals. She couldn't help but think it was an omen, as if fate was directing her.

And she knew all about fate from the way her mother had died so senselessly. They were all at the mercy of it. Fate gave and fate took away, but in the meantime everyone was in control of their own destiny, and somewhere along the line she had forgotten that.

Forgotten her desire for independence and self-reliance. She'd let herself imagine—or rather hope—that Zach was the man for her when really their whole relationship was built on an unfortunate set of circumstances instigated by her father.

Placing the broken petals of the orchid gently back on the table she turned to him.

'Then when the laws change we can—divorce?'

'We can do it now.' He strode through to his office and came back, slapping a document on the table beside her, squashing what remained of the flower of love. 'This is the legislation that gives you the freedom to apply for a divorce.' Picking up a pen, he signed it with a flourish before handing it to her.

Blindly she did so and handed it back. 'Congratulations,' he said, 'you can be the first woman in Bakaan to obtain a divorce. I'm sure you'll enjoy that.'

What she would enjoy would be if she had the freedom to go up to him, throw herself into his arms and kiss him. What she would enjoy would be for him to crush her to his hard length as he had done so many times before and tell her that he loved her…that he couldn't live without her.

She thought about her mother and the brother she had never known. She thought about her father who had desperately pined for them both and had held on to anger and bitterness when they had been ripped from him so unfairly. And then she thought about Zach who had wanted to marry for love and got her instead and she knew she was doing the honourable thing, the *only* thing, in walking away. 'So I think… I think I'd like to go home. If you don't mind.' *Did she have to sound like such a wimp?* 'To Al-Hajjar.'

She heard a loud crack in the quiet room and saw particles of the pen she had just held fall to the ground. 'I'm well aware that you have never considered the palace home, Farah,' Zach rasped. 'But unlike a mythical genie I can't rub a magic lamp and make it happen instantaneously.'

'I know that, Zach,' she said, struggling to keep the tremors out of her voice. 'I didn't mean…' Her explanation tapered off when she realised how close he was to her, how fiercely he was looking at her.

Kiss me, she urged silently. *Please.*

'I'll have Staph organise your transportation,' he said.

Farah pulled herself together. She smiled at him one last time and then, before her pride deserted her altogether, she left.

CHAPTER FIFTEEN

WHY DIDN'T ANYTHING work out the way you hoped it would? Zach growled under his breath as he wrestled with the cufflink he was currently trying to force back through his shirt sleeve.

'Would you stop fiddling?' Nadir berated out of the side of his mouth. 'You look like a schoolboy.'

Zach wanted to tell him in no uncertain terms where to go but they were at a formal gathering, waiting for the king of a neighbouring country to take his seat before they all could.

'And where's Farah? You said she'd be here. We don't want to insult this crusty old demon before he's signed the new business treaty.'

'I told you she's gone home,' Zach said.

Nadir frowned at him. 'That was a week ago. How long will she be gone?'

'How the hell do I know?' Finally the gold pin made it through the other side and, just when he went to twist the back into position, the damned thing fell out again. Zach swore just as the room held its breath for the old king to sit down.

All eyes turned his way. Nadir smiled. 'If you'll excuse us.' He nodded at Imogen and gave her a pointed look. Zach rolled his eye and went to take his seat when his brother cupped his elbow. 'You, outside.'

Zach nearly laughed as Nadir propelled him out of the room. 'Hell, I haven't been treated like a recalcitrant schoolboy since…well, since I was one.'

Nadir dismissed the nearby guards and walked ahead of him into an antechamber. 'What do you mean you don't know when Farah is due back? Didn't you ask her?'

No, he hadn't. He hadn't needed to ask to know that the answer was never. Instead he'd tried to forget about her and get on with his life.

Yeah, and wasn't that working out well?

He let his head drop back and started counting the small fretwork panels that decorated the ornate ceiling. He hadn't done that since he'd been a recalcitrant schoolboy either. 'She's on sabbatical.'

'Zach,' his brother said in *that* tone.

Zach blew out a breath. 'Do we really need to have this conversation now?' Because he was starving and a seven-course dinner was about to be served in the banquet hall.

His brother eyed him uncomfortably. 'I don't know. Do we?'

'Not in my mind.'

'Fine. But first tell me why you look worse than you did when you returned from your kidnapping in the desert.'

'I don't know. Perhaps I'm not getting my beauty sleep,' he quipped, deadpan.

Unfortunately Nadir didn't laugh. 'She left you, didn't she?'

'Who?'

'Damn it, Zach, I'm about—'

'Yes, she left me,' Zach grated. 'Happy?'

He stalked away from his brother and vaguely considered hurling an eighteenth-century Persian vase against the wall. It would probably shatter in a very satisfying manner.

'Want a drink?'

He hadn't heard Nadir go to the drinks cabinet and

he stared down at the two tumblers in his hand. 'No.' He didn't want a drink. He didn't want much of anything. The feeling of hollowness he'd experienced just after their father had died had returned tenfold.

'Fine. I'll have them both.'

Zach nearly laughed. His brother was trying to stage an intervention, and he loved him for it, but he was absolutely hopeless at the task.

Throwing himself into an armchair that was about as comfortable as a wooden plank, he regarded Nadir moodily. 'You probably should have told Imogen to come and talk to me instead.'

'Don't be an ass.' His brother took the other plank. 'So, what are you going to do about it?'

Zach looked at him bleakly. 'Nothing.'

'Well, that's healthy.'

'Listen, brother, I appreciate this, don't get me wrong—especially since you've ditched the King of Ormond for me—but my situation isn't like yours and Imogen's.'

'I don't know about that but what I do know is that you've finally found a woman you love and you're just going to let her go.'

Did he love her? This last week he'd convinced himself he didn't but that wasn't working out that well for him, either. 'I promised her I would.'

'Promised her what?'

'If you love something, you let it go. If it comes back, it was meant to be. If it doesn't, it never was.'

Nadir looked like he wanted to crack him over the head with one of the tumblers in his hand. 'If you love something you let it go...? That kind of drivel belongs in fairy tales and greeting cards, not in real life.'

'It was her decision. I'm not going to be like our father and chase her.'

Nadir sat forward and tilted a glass in his direction.

'I tell you, if you don't go to her and tell her how miserable you are without her, I will, because there's no way I'm losing one of the best regional ambassadors I'll probably ever have because you're too screwed up to tell her how you feel.'

'I'm not screwed up.'

But wasn't he?

A long buried memory rose up to taunt him as if it had happened yesterday. It was the day Nadir had argued with his father and left Bakaan for good. Being an eager-to-please thirteen-year-old on the cusp of manhood, Zach had wanted to make things right and had gone to his father and offered himself up as a replacement for Nadir. His father had stared at him for what had seemed like an eternity and then he'd started laughing. And he hadn't stopped until tears had rolled down his hollow cheeks and onto his white robe. Zach couldn't remember much of anything after that. The only thing he could remember was the hot ball of shame in his stomach as he'd stood before his father rooted to the spot.

Hell. He rubbed his hands over his face. He was so madly in love with Farah it had been easier to let her go than to open himself up to that kind of ridicule again. He looked back at his brother. 'Do you need the helicopter?'

'No.' Nadir shook his head. 'But take backup this time, will you? If her father doesn't shoot you out of the sky, your wife might, and with all the changes we're making we can't afford to replace it.'

Farah was tossing and turning in bed when she heard the distant sound of thunder.

Great. A storm was coming. At least she was home in her bed this time, her small, narrow bed that didn't seem to fit her any more. But then what would after the opulence of the Shomas Palace? Not that she missed the palace, exactly, but right now, when she could feel the coldness seeping in from outside, she missed the prince inside the palace. The prince she wasn't thinking about any more.

Slowly she became aware of voices outside her hut and the thunder that seemed to grow exponentially louder with every passing second. Thunder that was so loud it didn't sound like thunder at all.

Quickly climbing out of bed, she felt around on her chest of drawers for her trousers and tunic and slapped her boots against the floor before shoving her feet into them. Hopefully she wouldn't need socks because she didn't have time to look for any.

As soon as she stepped outside she had to put her hand up to shield her face from the circles of light surrounding their village—or what she realised were helicopters dropping from the sky like huge, black alien spaceships.

There was a sense of chaos amongst those who had been woken by the noise and Farah could see her father's men rallying to ward off any attack.

'Wait!' She rushed forward and shoved her way to the front of the gathering group. Her father was nowhere in sight but Amir looked set to kill.

She put her hand on his arm to stay him. They'd had a talk when she'd returned to the village a week ago and had fallen into an uneasy friendship, which basically meant that he avoided her at all costs. Something she completely understood.

What she didn't understand was why Zach was striding toward her, backlit by the now silent helicopters, his security team lined up behind him.

'Hello, Farah.'

Hello?

He invaded her village with an army and said hello? 'Zach? What are you doing here? Are you *trying* to start a war?'

'Not quite.' He stepped forward directly in front of her. 'I've come to talk to you.'

'At this time of the night?' Her heart was racing at the sight of him and she gave up trying to steady it. 'What could be so important it couldn't wait till morning?'

'Us. The future.'

The divorce. He was here about the divorce. Feeling completely stupid she took a moment to compose herself. 'Look,' she began haltingly, 'I haven't put the divorce petition into the court yet, but I will, I'm just—'

Zach took hold of her hands and she was embarrassed to feel them shaking. 'I'm not here about the divorce, *habiba.*' He squeezed her icy fingers. 'But what I have come to discuss I'd prefer to do so without an audience—or a line of guns trained on me. Is there somewhere private we can go?'

Wishing he had just sent a letter—or an emissary— to do his bidding she pulled out of his reach and glanced behind him. 'If you wanted private you shouldn't have brought a thousand men.'

'Only fifty.' He smiled ruefully. 'Nadir insisted on it.'

'What the blazes is this about, Darkhan?' Her father's sleep-roughened voice bellowed from behind them. Farah sighed as he pushed through the growing pack of villagers. So much for hoping her father might sleep through her final humiliation. He stopped in front of the prince. 'You have some nerve turning up like this.'

'Yes, sir. I've come for your daughter.'

Farah blinked, wondering if she had heard right.

'A man should know how to make his wife happy,' her father said. 'I made a promise to her mother many years ago that I would make sure she married well.'

Farah turned to him. 'You did?'

'Your mother said it would take a strong man to handle you. She was right. I never could.' He looked at Zach. 'That night in your shiny palace I saw something in your face when you looked at my daughter. Was I wrong?'

'No, sir. I love her.'

A murmur rippled through the crowd huddling together against the cold. Farah couldn't feel it. Heat was racing through her on a wave of embarrassment. 'By Allah.' She turned to her father. 'He doesn't love me. He's just saying that because—' She frowned, turning back to Zach. 'Why are you saying that?'

He smiled. 'Because it's true.'

'You love me?'

'With all my heart.'

'But...you were forced to marry me. My father—'

'Thinks you need to take this inside,' he said gruffly, directing them both towards the hut. 'And perhaps you should come and see me afterwards, Your Highness,' her father hesitated, 'about that other business.'

Did he mean the kidnapping?

'No, need sir. And the name's Zach.'

Her father nodded once. 'Mohamed.'

Shaking with the rush of emotions surging through her, Farah let Zach lead her inside her home, part of her desperate to play it safe and send him away and part of her aching to believe him.

'Our marriage was forced on the both of us, Farah, but there is nothing forced about the way I feel about you or how miserable I've been since you left.' He cupped her face in his hands and bent to kiss her with such tenderness it made her heart catch. 'I love you, *habiba*. I was just too much of a coward to tell you. And I have to believe that after the way you gave yourself to me, after everything that we shared together, that you have feelings for me, too. That you'll come back to me and give our marriage another chance.'

'Oh, Zach.' A lump formed in her throat as she looked

up at him. She had tried to avoid the pain of love her whole life, yet that was all she had felt since she had walked away from him. Deep down she knew that if she didn't take this leap of faith, that if she didn't fight the insecurities that had made her feel less than her whole life she would never know the joy of truly living. 'I love you, too. I love you so much I can't believe it. I can't—' She stopped talking and kissed him until they were both breathless and dizzy.

'I love you, Farah. I didn't know it was possible to love someone this much.'

'But you let me go.'

'You asked me to and I had given you my word that if you ever wanted to leave then I would not come after you.'

Farah groaned. 'That would be one of the only times you've ever done what I asked.'

'Not true. In Ibiza I did everything you asked. I watched cheesy movies for you.'

'But why were you so distant these past few weeks? I thought it was because you wanted a way out of our marriage. That you were starting to resent it. To resent me.'

He gathered her close and kissed her again, kissed her until she couldn't think. 'I didn't resent you but I could tell you were holding something back and I didn't know how to reach out to you.' He sighed and stroked his thumbs across her cheekbones. 'The truth is, I wanted you so badly I started to doubt myself.'

'You?'

'Yes, me.' He gave her a wry smile. 'Love, I have learned, is not the comfortable, easy emotion I had once envisioned. It's hot and powerful and it brought me to my knees. You brought me to my knees.'

Farah stroked her hand over his stubble, revelling in the fact that she could touch him freely. 'You know, when we first met you annoyed me so much I wanted to do exactly that.'

He smiled. 'Is that a fact? You should be careful what you wish for, *habiba*...'

'Because you just might get it.' She laughed. 'I'm so happy, Zach. I never thought I would feel like this with a man.'

He pulled her in tighter against him. 'You don't feel like this with *a man*. You feel like this with *me*.'

A secret smile formed on her lips. 'So that self-doubt you were talking about...?'

'A blip on the radar. A blip that you have eradicated.'

'I'm glad,' she said, suddenly serious. 'And I'm glad you changed your mind about coming after me. Because without you...without you...'

Tears formed on the ends of her lashes and he used his thumbs to wipe them away. 'You are my destiny, Farah.' He leaned back to look down at her. 'You're the reason I returned to Bakaan five years ago and you're the reason I no longer want to leave. You light up my life, *habiba*, in a way I've been looking for my whole life and never thought I'd find.'

'Oh, Zach, take me home,' she whispered.

'To the palace?'

'To wherever you are.' She curled her hands around his neck. 'I never want to be parted from you again.'

'Good. Because I never plan to let you go again.'

He sealed his promise with a soul deep kiss that was filled with joy and the promise of a wonderful future, and Farah knew that her mighty prince was truly a man she could rely on for the rest of her life.

* * * * *

MILLS & BOON®
Hardback – October 2015

ROMANCE

Claimed for Makarov's Baby	Sharon Kendrick
An Heir Fit for a King	Abby Green
The Wedding Night Debt	Cathy Williams
Seducing His Enemy's Daughter	Annie West
Reunited for the Billionaire's Legacy	Jennifer Hayward
Hidden in the Sheikh's Harem	Michelle Conder
Resisting the Sicilian Playboy	Amanda Cinelli
The Return of Antonides	Anne McAllister
Soldier, Hero...Husband?	Cara Colter
Falling for Mr December	Kate Hardy
The Baby Who Saved Christmas	Alison Roberts
A Proposal Worth Millions	Sophie Pembroke
The Baby of Their Dreams	Carol Marinelli
Falling for Her Reluctant Sheikh	Amalie Berlin
Hot-Shot Doc, Secret Dad	Lynne Marshall
Father for Her Newborn Baby	Lynne Marshall
His Little Christmas Miracle	Emily Forbes
Safe in the Surgeon's Arms	Molly Evans
Pursued	Tracy Wolff
A Royal Temptation	Charlene Sands

MILLS & BOON®
Large Print – October 2015

ROMANCE

The Bride Fonseca Needs	Abby Green
Sheikh's Forbidden Conquest	Chantelle Shaw
Protecting the Desert Heir	Caitlin Crews
Seduced into the Greek's World	Dani Collins
Tempted by Her Billionaire Boss	Jennifer Hayward
Married for the Prince's Convenience	Maya Blake
The Sicilian's Surprise Wife	Tara Pammi
His Unexpected Baby Bombshell	Soraya Lane
Falling for the Bridesmaid	Sophie Pembroke
A Millionaire for Cinderella	Barbara Wallace
From Paradise...to Pregnant!	Kandy Shepherd

HISTORICAL

A Mistress for Major Bartlett	Annie Burrows
The Chaperon's Seduction	Sarah Mallory
Rake Most Likely to Rebel	Bronwyn Scott
Whispers at Court	Blythe Gifford
Summer of the Viking	Michelle Styles

MEDICAL

Just One Night?	Carol Marinelli
Meant-To-Be Family	Marion Lennox
The Soldier She Could Never Forget	Tina Beckett
The Doctor's Redemption	Susan Carlisle
Wanted: Parents for a Baby!	Laura Iding
His Perfect Bride?	Louisa Heaton

MILLS & BOON®
Hardback – November 2015

ROMANCE

A Christmas Vow of Seduction	Maisey Yates
Brazilian's Nine Months' Notice	Susan Stephens
The Sheikh's Christmas Conquest	Sharon Kendrick
Shackled to the Sheikh	Trish Morey
Unwrapping the Castelli Secret	Caitlin Crews
A Marriage Fit for a Sinner	Maya Blake
Larenzo's Christmas Baby	Kate Hewitt
Bought for Her Innocence	Tara Pammi
His Lost-and-Found Bride	Scarlet Wilson
Housekeeper Under the Mistletoe	Cara Colter
Gift-Wrapped in Her Wedding Dress	Kandy Shepherd
The Prince's Christmas Vow	Jennifer Faye
A Touch of Christmas Magic	Scarlet Wilson
Her Christmas Baby Bump	Robin Gianna
Winter Wedding in Vegas	Janice Lynn
One Night Before Christmas	Susan Carlisle
A December to Remember	Sue MacKay
A Father This Christmas?	Louisa Heaton
A Christmas Baby Surprise	Catherine Mann
Courting the Cowboy Boss	Janice Maynard

MILLS & BOON®
Large Print – November 2015

ROMANCE

The Ruthless Greek's Return	Sharon Kendrick
Bound by the Billionaire's Baby	Cathy Williams
Married for Amari's Heir	Maisey Yates
A Taste of Sin	Maggie Cox
Sicilian's Shock Proposal	Carol Marinelli
Vows Made in Secret	Louise Fuller
The Sheikh's Wedding Contract	Andie Brock
A Bride for the Italian Boss	Susan Meier
The Millionaire's True Worth	Rebecca Winters
The Earl's Convenient Wife	Marion Lennox
Vettori's Damsel in Distress	Liz Fielding

HISTORICAL

A Rose for Major Flint	Louise Allen
The Duke's Daring Debutante	Ann Lethbridge
Lord Laughraine's Summer Promise	Elizabeth Beacon
Warrior of Ice	Michelle Willingham
A Wager for the Widow	Elisabeth Hobbes

MEDICAL

Always the Midwife	Alison Roberts
Midwife's Baby Bump	Susanne Hampton
A Kiss to Melt Her Heart	Emily Forbes
Tempted by Her Italian Surgeon	Louisa George
Daring to Date Her Ex	Annie Claydon
The One Man to Heal Her	Meredith Webber

MILLS & BOON®

Why shop at millsandboon.co.uk?

Each year, thousands of romance readers find their perfect read at millsandboon.co.uk. That's because we're passionate about bringing you the very best romantic fiction. Here are some of the advantages of shopping at www.millsandboon.co.uk:

* **Get new books first**—you'll be able to buy your favourite books one month before they hit the shops

* **Get exclusive discounts**—you'll also be able to buy our specially created monthly collections, with up to 50% off the RRP

* **Find your favourite authors**—latest news, interviews and new releases for all your favourite authors and series on our website, plus ideas for what to try next

* **Join in**—once you've bought your favourite books, don't forget to register with us to rate, review and join in the discussions

Visit **www.millsandboon.co.uk**
for all this and more today!